A Taste of Honey

ALSO BY KAI ASHANTE WILSON

The Sorcerer of the Wildeeps
"The Devil in America"
"Super Bass"

A TASTE

OF

HONEY

KAI ASHANTE WILSON

A TOM DOHERTY ASSOCIATES BOOK

NEW YORK

This is a work of fiction. All of the characters, organizations, and events portrayed in this novella are either products of the author's imagination or are used fictitiously.

A TASTE OF HONEY

Copyright © 2016 by Kai Ashante Wilson

Cover art by Tommy Arnold
Cover designed by Christine Foltzer

Edited by Carl Engle-Laird

A Tor.com Book
Published by Tom Doherty Associates
175 Fifth Avenue
New York, NY 10010

www.tor.com

Tor® is a registered trademark of Macmillan Publishing Group, LLC.

ISBN 978-0-7653-9005-9 (ebook)
ISBN 978-0-7653-9004-2 (trade paperback)

First Edition: October 2016

For Anna S.
Thank you for opening my eyes
to new dimensions of thought, feeling, and art.

Part One

The little dark songbirds will come again;
though not exactly those that paused in flight,
captivated by your beauty and my happiness,
and learned both our names—those
shall never come again.

Gustavo Adolfo Bécquer

Backlit in the bright doorway, a silhouette shouted into the nighttime street: "Hey beautiful," and the foreign soldier called again. "Hey!"

Aqib glanced over his shoulder. A man should glimpse, shouldn't he, when some lovely woman is walking just behind? But no one followed nearby on the boulevard.

"*No—*" Resplendent in his breastplate, the Daluçan soldier walked out into the dappled moonlight under the border trees. "*—You,* man. So beautiful!"

Startled, Aqib laughed. Girls of marriageable age, and their aunty-brokers, often told him so these days, but never yet a man. Far more than either his sister or brother, Aqib resembled their mother, closely reprising her exotic features. Always-Walking-People from the north tended to smallness of frame and stature—and from them his aquiline nose, and a glossy excess of hair no scissors had ever yet checked. Freed just this morning from braids, the heavy tangle of it billowed around his head like ram's wool.

"*Vale, Dalucianus,*" he said, hailing the soldier with words from beyond the sea, and then strode on with a wave. But the soldier called back, "No, wait up!" so Aqib halted in the road, the cat beside him, crouching on her haunches while the soldier approached.

For a full season, the king's heralds had cried through the City's streets just how all Olorumi, whether of the Blood or salt of the earth, were to treat with the embassy from Daluz once the foreigners arrived: rendering the Daluçans every honor, and offending none of them, on any account. Aqib had heard these things, of course, from his own father: "I know you shall be gracious at the fêtes, my boy, always warm and forthcoming; for I do not doubt that you will be called upon to give some performance for them. And to any Daluçan you meet in passing, extend the utmost courtesy, that they should know only comfort, only welcome, here in Great Olorum. Have I spoken clearly, Aqib-sa?"

"Oh, you *have*, Papa," Aqib had said. "Yes, Master Sadiqi!"

The soldier met him eye to eye. So, a man of only middling height; but he wasn't slightly built, nor with a bird's bones. The Daluçan was broad-shouldered and stout-muscled as Aqib's own brother, and male cousins: warriors all. And when the soldier emerged from leaf-shadows under the bordering trees, into the clarity mid-boulevard, the features of his face showed unweathered and young. Like the lyric, his head was "a night without stars," which was to say, without a single pale strand compromising the darkness of his hair. Aqib guessed that he and this soldier were of an age, more or less: past a half-man's initiation at fifteen years old, not yet come to a full-man's at twenty-five.

"*Servus, pulchre!* I'm—" Then the soldier saw, properly, the animal crouched beside Aqib. He jumped back with a yelp. "Whoa, that ain't no dog!"

"No." Aqib patted the cat's head. She leaned against him, pressing her fuzzy skull to his hand. "She's the favorite cat of the prince, who is Blessèd among Olorumi," said Aqib. All day she'd run hard, and taken down two antelope, and gorged herself. Now she was in drowsy sweet temper. "Her name is Sabah."

"I thought that was a big *dog*." The soldier drew near again. "So, they just let you walk free around the City with your long skinny lion?"

"Cheetah," Aqib said; "and she belongs to the Blest, not to me. It's my responsibility to take her down to the Royal Park to run and hunt when the prince is too much occupied. But there's no cause for worry, believe me. Sabah's used to people. I sat right beside her dam, the morning Sabah came to light in the Royal Menagerie. I know she will not hurt you."

"Not 'less you sic her on me," the soldier said insistently. "I'd be shit outta luck *then*, if you said, 'Go on, girl. Get that soldier-man right there. Eat him up!'"

Aqib was shocked. "I would *never* do such a thing." And he lay a hand of emphatic reassurance on the soldier's arm.

. . . belatedly realizing the man had only been making fun. Still, Aqib's expression or tone of voice—the touch?—caused the soldier to look at him no longer mockingly, but with some friendlier feeling. The soldier's forearm was crisscrossed by weapons' scars. Aqib felt thews hard and articulate as carved teakwood; sweat-damp, downed with fine hair . . . It seemed almost as if that smile and gaze invited Aqib to leave it put when he withdrew his hand.

"So you take care of the Blest's cat, huh?" the soldier said. "Does that make you somebody important?"

"No. Well, yes—perhaps so. I am a fourth-order Cousin of the Blood, and my father is Master of Beasts and the Hunt for the king. And now I hope you will excuse me, but I *really* ought to have got Sabah back to the Menagerie already."

"Care if I walk with you? The rest of the Embassy's up at the palace thataway. And I hardly ever seen such a beautiful"—the soldier grinned, eyetooth missing just where some scar nicked his upper lip—"night as this."

Gallant, this soldier from Daluz! And he really was quite handsome, too, in a wildly foreign sort of way; probably full of exciting stories. "Of course you may accompany us," Aqib said; and as they began walking together, he thoughtlessly quoted the lay of Saintly Canon spoken by a royal daughter when, at her moment of greatest danger, her Sainted paladin makes a timely appearance: "'We were all alone, and so do greet you with a glad heart; for the protection of a strong man tells, when perils of the lonely night threaten.'" *Absurd* thing to say! Aqib ducked his head. Why was his tongue so foolish?

The Daluçan whooped with laughter. "No threats and dangers here in Olorum, that I can see," he said. "Guess what? Back home in Terra-de-Luce, we got gangs of bandits running loose right in the city streets. Anyhow, I left my *gladium* back at the palace. But you have that big knife on your belt there. *You* watch out for us."

"Oh, no, *Dalucianus!*" Aqib said. "This? It's only a bush-knife: for the hunt, butchering prey, field mercy, and so forth. I am no warrior"—the old upset began to trouble Aqib's voice, wrack his countenance, and he had to calm himself—"though my brother is, and my cousins are. I myself cannot show even one war scar. So, whatever perils we face, salvation will not come from me." Aqib looked over the soldier who walked beside him. *Here* was every inch a warrior!

Some arrowpoint had once clipped the soldier's forehead, leaving a pale gouge in the dark arc of his left brow. The Daluçan's undertunic and gleaming breastplate left his arms bare: both countlessly scored by scratches, a few new-red, many long healed. Down his right forearm, however, a knotty length of cicatrix, the remnants of a dreadful wound, snaked from elbow to wrist. It had plainly been won in the thick of battle, and the sight of this badge of manhood, so bravely borne, put Aqib quite into his place: a mere boy. It acted as a sort of rebuke, even; for Aqib's own flesh was entirely undecorated from head to toe. Nothing on him was—to use the soldier's term—so beautiful. Abashed, Aqib tore his gaze from the scar.

The soldier was looking at him strangely. "I forgot about that. How you Olorumi admire wounds, like they're the mark of a man. Well, nobody looks at 'em that way where I come from. . . . Hey, what's your name? Oh, 'Aqib'—I like that! Where I come from, Aqib, the thing we love is smooth unmarked skin, like yours." While he spoke, the soldier frowned and rubbed self-consciously at the old scar on his right arm, as if such proof of hero-ism could in any way be shameful.

They'd misunderstood each other somehow, Aqib re-alized. Without intending it, he'd offered the Daluçan some offense. He couldn't think what next to say safely.

"Now looky there." It was the soldier who spoke first. "See those flowers and glow bugs? That's sure *'nough* pretty!"

Indeed it was. And one could, in all safety, bang on about the weather forever. "The season of Long Rains draws nigh," Aqib explained. "For you can see that the moonflowers are coming into blossom. And those, prop-erly speaking, are called night-bees."

Alongside the boulevard, there was a whole length of hedge round some rich merchant's compound blooming. Night-bees swarmed over the huge blowsy flowers, white phosphoresced in the moonlight. As drafts cause candle-wicks to brighten, so did the glimmering of the nights-bees flare while they drank nectar, then dim at liftoff to the next blossom.

Sabah stopped to drink at a public fountain. They must drink from the clean water in the upper basins,

Aqib explained; for poor folk bathed and laundered clothes in the lower pool. The Daluçan ducked his whole head under the downward cascade. When he came up, he said, "You don't wear a man's robes, Aqib." The soldier's wet hair had slicked down otterishly to contours of his skull. "Why's that?"

"Oh, I prefer boy's clothes," Aqib said, and played out one long tendril from the flat soaked pelt atop the Daluçan's head. The soldier stilled for this examination with a bemused smile. "Though as a Cousin of the Blood, I may wear majority's robes at any age." Aqib, however, persisted in the shirt and trousers of a youth. "My father hasn't chosen a wife for me yet, so there's still a little time to do as I please."

"Yeah?" the soldier said. "I thought you Olorumi picked your own husband or wife."

"It often happens that way," Aqib said. Sabah now jumped in the fountain to wallow. "My father and my brother both married for love. But my mother wasn't of the Blood, so that marriage greatly lowered our family's standing. Master Sadiqi wants a second-order Cousin for me, at least. Some woman who can lift us high at court again."

"And what about you? There must be a girl you care for better than the rest. Who's the prettiest one?"

"*Ehn.*" Aqib waved a vague hand. He bent his head

and cupped up drinking water from the fountain's higher basin.

The soldier gave a crack of laughter, as if at some good joke.

Aqib looked up, startled. Well, *all* the daughters of the court who vied for him were very pretty, he explained. *Everyone* told him so!

This only made the soldier laugh the more hearty. "Most men, Aqib, don't need somebody else to explain which woman's beautiful!"

Chilling words to Aqib, even a little frightening; for manhood's ways had often tripped him up, and his errors provoked harsh correction. But he saw and heard nothing cruel, nothing angry, in the Daluçan's laughter. You can feel when someone takes delight in you, and Aqib felt that, so it seemed all right. He relaxed and smiled again. However Master Sadiqi chose, Aqib explained, he would be content to do his duty. Sabah jumped from the fountain and shook herself with a drenching spatter. They walked on, Aqib chattering about the weather.

Nights before the Long Rains opened, a very sweet and particular breeze blew in the spell between dusk and morning. Those airs refreshed, much cooler than the normal swelter. They bore scents so ripe, of fecundity and flowers, that Olorumi named these winds green. Just such a green wind was blowing now. Could *Dalucianus* not feel the freshness, smell it? "It's certain the Long Rains will open in much less than one month," Aqib said. "Yes. For you can see—right there, see?—that heaven is clouding over already."

"It ain't." The soldier said, looking up. "I hardly seen a sky so bright with stars."

Nor *did* the firmament lack for brightness, but Aqib put an arm round the soldier and turned him about—west—pointing out where obscurities in heaven's lower strata had blotted black tracts across the night's starry prospect. "Now do you see? Those are the first wet clouds of the Long Rains, gathering in the upper airs."

At first the soldier nodded, staring where the finger pointed, and then quietly looked to Aqib, who felt his face flush, and the breath catch in his throat. How close they stood! He'd thought Daluçans touched as freely as Olorumi; but some fraught quality arose from the arm he'd put about the soldier. It was so hard to tell another people's mores! Aqib let his arm fall away.

To win back to the lighter mood of before, Aqib began to speak of his siblings, his father, the folk of his household.

The Daluçan said, "So your father picked *you* then—not your brother, not your sister—to be his heir? Even though you're the baby."

"Oh!" Aqib had never quite conceived of the matter in this manner. "Well, I wouldn't say . . . It's better to say, I think, that only *one* of us had aptitude and vocation, both. My brother lacks the . . . rapport, I suppose you could say, to work well with animals. All he cares for, anyway, is to make a distinguished career in the armies. My sister . . . ? Ha! Our great-grandmother *built* the Menagerie, but my sister is a very exquisite sort of woman. She *abhors* mess. Papa had hoped she might pursue medicine and help out at the Menagerie, but Sister absolutely refused. Nothing but the cleanliest of womanly arts for *her*! Physicals and mathematicals, and so forth." Aqib made the shooing motion males employ for mysteries belonging to the female sex.

"Physics and maths," said the Daluçan.

"Mmm, yes," Aqib said, and then, marveling, turned to the soldier. "Your knowledge of my language is remarkably broad: even the *girl* words! But your accent, your manner of speech is"—low-rent, uncouth—"*interesting*. Who taught you to speak Olorumi?"

"This sailor I knew, who used to ship on a freighter of your king's argosy. Dude could hardly speak two words of Daluçan, so I learned your guys' talk off him."

To acknowledge some value of "learned," Aqib nodded attentively.

"We were . . . friends, for a couple years," the soldier

said and looked away. Sabah licked the fingers of the hand the Daluçan extended to her. Then the cat turned to sniff some beast's dung left in the road. "I kept asking him to settle with me in Daluz, but he loved voyaging and the sea *way* more than . . . Anyway, he sailed off one day and never came back. Later on, I heard that his ship went down in a storm, out in the Uttermost East." The soldier glanced at Aqib, glanced away again.

Aqib didn't quite understand the depth of feeling here, but he spoke the cliché, the formula phrase: "It is hard—it hurts us very deeply, doesn't it?—to lose those whom we love most."

"*Yes.*" The soldier looked at Aqib with sudden respect, as if they now shared an understanding. "It was *real* hard. Nothing ever hurt me worse. But that's how I got asked to come on the embassy—because I know your guys' talk so good. Me, I'm just a centurion of the cavalry, but the others are all *semidivini* knights. Most of *them,* though, hardly speak a word of Olorumi."

"That's of no matter." Aqib waved off this concern. "We all, every Cousin of the court, speaks *excellent* Daluçan."

The soldier grinned. "Not really, Aqib. You palace-types think your talk is so good, but . . . Like '*vale*' means farewell, so you should of said '*salve*' for hello. And when you're talking right at somebody, it's '*Daluciane,*' not '*Dalucianus.*' Understand?"

Aqib's face stiffened with embarrassment, but his manners didn't fail. "Yes," he said evenly. "Thank you. I shall remember."

Drawn by gulf buffalo, a night wagon trundled past them: its benches brimming over with men and women, burly or sinewy, who stank and sang, drunk. Obviously they were all poor laborers, momentarily rich—lately back from a season's work across-bayou on the gods' estates. Riff-raff!

"I see you'd sooner go on foot," said the soldier merrily. The merriment owing to the vast disdain, Aqib realized, showing plain upon his face.

Although high born, one needn't go round haughtily *seeming* so; Aqib quickly fixed his expression. "Of course it's *wonderful* that the gods employ so many from Olorum on their estates. The food those menials grow, and the wealth they bring back cross-bayou to the Kingdom, has helped to make us Olorumi the richest and most prosperous of the world's peoples"—true, but was that quite the *politic* thing to say, Aqib?—"though, naturally, the wonders of Daluz, your nation's prowess at war, for instance, and the storied loveliness of your cities, have no match upon the sphere."

The soldier laughed. "We're for sure no courtiers, us two! Aqib, it really ain't no need for you to get all mealy-mouth on *my* account." It was such a nice laugh. Just as

I do, Aqib thought, he lacks the forked or silver tongue necessary at court. Plain speech won't offend him.

Wishing to test this insight, and with his usual precipitation of thought into action, Aqib said provocatively:

"You are aware the negotiations on this side of the bayou, between us mortals of Daluz and Olorum, are not the ones of true import?" Watching askance for reaction, Aqib flicked away a night-bee that lit upon the soldier's head, creeping in his hair. "Careful; they pinch."

"Thanks. Yeah, I know," the soldier said peaceably. "Ours is just the little business—your wootz and diamonds, our Pax Daluciana and war arts." The soldier obliged with good humor as Aqib's fingers satisfied their curiosity in his now-dry hair. "But over there cross-bayou, our gods are talking to yours about the big stuff. You know what the gods want, right?"

"I do. I cannot claim to understand it, but I know their aim."

"Well, our gods of Daluz think they can get it, finally, if your gods will marry in, and make both bloods stronger."

Aqib took his hand from the soldier's hair. "So I've heard." That cowlick just wouldn't lie flat. "Oh, look. Here we are—the Menagerie."

Some way back, the City's houses and tenements had thinned in favor of lots of urban pasturage and gardens. And there looming on the most humongous of these lots was the Menagerie. The Daluçan made an expansive gesture. "What's that around it? *Vallum aut silva?*"

"Hmm, well . . ." Aqib, seeing that the soldier was staggered by the sight, took in afresh this place he'd known all his life. "I suppose it's both, rather: fort *and* forest. Would you like a quick tour?"

"Yeah! If that's all right . . ."

Inwalling the Menagerie was a palisade not possibly built by mortal means. The serried boles of hardwood trees grew impassably close, the green canopies interleaved together high above: this wall wholly alive except for the carpentered gates, over which a godslight floated, its bluish glare harsh enough to vanquish a wide swath of night. Aqib led soldier and cat off the boulevard, into the actinic illumination under the gates.

And brighter be the light, then deeper the shadows: one errant branch, immensely jutting from a palisade-tree, threw a patch of blackness upon the ground. Hidden in that dark, someone called out: "*Aqib bmg Sadiqi?*"—an inescapable voice, all too well known. "Is that you, brother, with your wild hair?" Three men came swaggering from shadow, toting weighty battle-spears. The speaker, whom one must never address as other than "Corporal," said, "Who is that with you? I do not know that stranger." The three men wore robes of majority and armor-plated jerkins. Without exception, they were formidable in stature, breadth of shoulder, strength of arm.

"Be at ease, I pray you, Corporal," Aqib said, and took the Daluçan soldier's hand, as he might a close friend's. "Come with me to see the Menagerie is one from Daluz. We Olorumi swore safe passage to all of the Daluçan Embassy, and we swore it by the blood of every Saint. I ask you, then, to proffer greetings to this man."

"*Vale, Dalucianus,*" said the Corporal grudgingly, echoed by his two fellows. The three enjoyed a good hard stare at this soldier from so far abroad: the pallor of his skin seeming moreso under the godslight, his hair lank as a horsetail. They looked especially at the steel-alloy breastplate he wore, its dazzling mirror-polish. The Corporal, taking some steps from the other guardsmen, beckoned to Aqib: "Come here, brother. I wish to drop a word in your ear."

The Daluçan soldier squeezed Aqib's hand and let go. "Go 'head. I'm right here waiting for you."

Worriedly Aqib looked between the man beside him and the Corporal. "I won't be a moment. Sabah, stay. Stay put, girl."

Across Aqib's shoulders, the Corporal lay a powerful arm and, whispering, pulled him in close. "Be wary, Aqib," the Corporal said. "Do nothing to disrespect our family's honor, do you hear? Where that one comes from, they know nothing of righteousness, nothing of the Saints. The Daluçans follow ... other ways. Do you take my meaning?"

No. " ... yes?" said Aqib; and frightened of his brother, he began as usual to babble. "But I am sure there is no cause for worry. Sabah can always smell out bad intentions. Remember that thief, and the assassin? *Him,* she doesn't mind in the least. She knows a bright soul. Look there; she lets him pat her head! I am sure the Daluçan means no harm. He is *very* friendly."

"I daresay he is, you silly wretch!" The Corporal ground his teeth together. "You must have some notion, Aqib, of the *turpitudes of luxury* that go on in the wide world beyond Olorum—such unspeakable acts as *never* should occur! Don't you see?"

Aqib felt now as he had all throughout childhood: that everyone was moving deftly within norms long established, confidently speaking in terms already defined, but that no one had remembered to clue in poor little Aqib. "Please, I beg you, Brother ... ," he began. "*Corporal,* I mean to say!" He hurriedly corrected himself. "I cannot understand you. What do you mean?"

"By our own Sainted mother! You *don't* know, do you?" The Corporal's arm squeezed Aqib round the neck, shook him roughly. "Such a spoilt, sheltered child you are!" The Corporal seemed fit to burst with the desire to explain further. In the end, though, as if to himself, he only quoted Canon: "'An the mantle be immaculate, cast no filth upon it.'" He then repeated himself. "Do *nothing* to disrespect our family's honor."

"I wouldn't." Aqib promised. "I never will."

"You all good, over here? Everything all right?"

Startled by this irruption, the Corporal flung Aqib aside to clear a space for his spear. Aqib might have fallen, but the Daluçan soldier caught and bore him up. His body pressed uncomfortably for a moment to the metallic chest, his mouth and nose to the bearded neck; then the corded arm released him, except for a hand. One *cannot* love a new friend more than one's own brother, or should not anyway.

The Corporal glowered, his fists clenched about his spear. Although taller, he wasn't half so heavily built as the Daluçan—beside whom Aqib felt himself able to stand uncowed for once, even with his brother looking daggers. Aqib knew that he embodied shortfall, disappointment, and inadequacy; still, though, how had he ever trespassed so far as to merit the hatred burning in the Corporal's eyes?

"All is well, *Dalucianus,*" said the Corporal. "And as for you, Brother, I pray to see you ever abiding by the Saintly Canon. Our good father came by the Menagerie this afternoon. Master Sadiqi was *not* best pleased to find you neglecting the bears. His very words: 'That boy has work enough here to do. These jaunts with Sabah can wait.'"

"But how should the prince's favorite cat," Aqib exclaimed, "be kept always in her pen and fed dead meat, day after day, with no joy of the field—?" He cut himself off. When calm, his speech was melodious and modulated, a sweet tenor; but when upset, his voice took just that note of girlish stridence no man can take seriously. More calmly Aqib went on. "The prince himself bade me take Sabah often to the Royal Park."

Smirking, the Corporal only lifted his shoulders and dropped them. *You argue with the wrong one. I do but deliver the message.*

Aqib nodded. "Very well. I shall do just as Master Sadiqi our father requires, of course." And he went to the gates, gave the sign—whistling the note—that undid the lock, and opened the wicket door, letting himself, Sabah, and the soldier inside.

And what was inside?

Stink.

Noise!

From the godslight without, fractured brightness pierced the wooden gates, and these scattered rays picked out a bewildering labyrinth of split-rail corrals and stout wickerwork cages, some of which were piddling hutches stacked one atop another, rodents inside, or piglets, or coneys; other cages so vastly built as to encompass a stunted tree, rocky hillock, or small pond. The yips of hunting coyotes, snuffles of hippopotamus, blown breath of equines, of antelopes, and all manner of simian gibbering came from the divers enclosures.

"Oh, my menials have done *poor work* today!" Aqib led Sabah and the Daluçan down pungent, noisy straits. "Whenever I spend the afternoon at the Park it's like this! They will muck, they will gather it up into piles, but they will *not* cart the shit out to the gardens . . . ! Tomorrow there shall be a reckoning, oh yes— Careful!" Aqib leapt forward, pulling hard upon the soldier's hand still in his own. The Daluçan staggered after him. Briefly cloying the air, a glob of rotted plantain winged past, just missing them. "The chimps," Aqib explained. "I do apologize. Up you go, Sabah." They'd stopped beside a fence densely woven of living bushes. "Go on now!" And Sabah sprang nimbly onto the fence, scrabbled to the top, whence she jumped down, disappearing inside.

"She could get out of there easy enough, look to me."

"Certainly. But Sabah's a good girl. She'll stay put." Just then a little coolness pattered Aqib's scalp, neck and shoulder, like tiny pinpricks, and he turned his face heavenward. A drop splashed his forehead, another his chin, and then no more.

"*O Daluciane!* Did you feel that? The clouds just now

gave their first taste of the Long Rains!"

"Yeah, I felt it," the soldier said. And the same bright grin communicated between them.

"You have it in your mind," Aqib said, jubilant, "that Olorum is green already. But we *aren't* yet. No, right now we are parched: we are withered and almost dead. But only wait until after the Long Rains have drenched us city and nation—*then* you were in Paradise, my friend! Wait and see!"

"*Eheu, amicissime,*" the soldier said with a sad smile; "*nam ego dies decem solos hic manebo. Me deinde ultra mare reperies. Illud numquam miraculum videbo.*"

The giddy joy bled away. "Oh," Aqib said. "Only ten days more. I had quite forgot. Of course you've already been here this whole long season. I wish . . . I wish we had met on the first day of your arrival, instead of so near your leave-taking."

"Me, too," the Daluçan said. "I feel the exact same way, Aqib."

They stood side by side at the elephants': watching the mother beast work upon one of the enclosure's godtrees, tearing away leafy acacia branches, knocking loose apples, so that food fell down within reach of her baby.

Aqib began to expound: "A godtree—"

"We've got us a few godtrees, Aqib," the soldier said, "even in far-off Daluz."

"Oh yes," Aqib said, "of course, you do." One never knew quite what needed explaining, and where the silences should go.

A chance lull in the cries of the animals carried to them laughter from the Corporal and guardsmen out front, making boasts and curses as they threw bones together. Aqib would *never* stand as a peer to such men, however long he lived, whatever he accomplished: suddenly he knew the truth of this to his very bones. At that moment, Aqib felt he could bear anything in the world better than more hateful sneers and bitter words from his brother. Yet he and the Daluçan would have to pass the gauntlet at the gate again. Master Sadiqi had of course shown him the secret way through the walls surrounding the Menagerie. But Aqib was mindful of the great confidence invested in him, and no one else alive; surely it wouldn't do to go revealing the secret passage to an outsider, even one of bright soul? The soldier, leaning close, spoke softly: "Could I kiss you, Aqib?"

"No!" Aqib answered, shocked, whispering himself. "Men *cannot* kiss!" Yet it seemed there was a conspiracy within his own body. For it took all of his strength not to consummate their nearness into actual touch, while he was utterly strengthless to shift even an inch away.

"I bet you they can." The soldier's breath smelled of young palm wine. "Anybody ever make love to you,

Aqib?" So near, his words were sensation, a brush of feathers. "Let me; I want to. Can I?"

A mystery clarified for Aqib, and not just concerning this long walk, this fraught conversation—not just tonight's mystery, as it were—but the deeper one concerning his inmost self. Ah, *this* was why his wayward gaze alit so often on whom it shouldn't, going back to peek howevermuch snatched away: those taut bellies and hard thighs of men heroically scrawled in scars. So yes, then: *clearly* two men could kiss! And what else might they do? Lie down together kissing, if they both wished it, and furthermore . . . *unclothed*? A desperate thrill of desire throbbed in Aqib's loins, nearly a climax. "No," he whispered harshly, seizing the soldier's wrist in a staying grip. "We *cannot,* for Saintly Recitature says . . . And we are in the open here." Nervously he glanced back toward the front gate of the Menagerie, whence again came the sound of laughter. "My brother . . ." would *kill* us, or try to. The very earth seemed to list and yaw, when Aqib thought of the Corporal's face deranged by fury, raining down unstoppable violence.

"What about inside then, Aqib? Where nobody could see us? I can take a room back at that *taberna.* I hate it up at the Sovereign House, anyway. Everybody in the palace hustling one bill of goods or the other. Come with me back to the place where we met."

Yes, all right! Let's go now—and we'll leave by the secret door!

But in an aggrieved tone, postponing this decision, Aqib said, "How can I? I do not even know your name, O Soldier of Daluz."

He smiled. "We can fix that, easy. I'll tell you. My name is—"

[*ELEVENTH DAY*]

Great Olorum gathered at the seashore to see off the Daluçan ship. In formal robes he stood among his father, sister, and brother in the shade afforded by their house parasolists. The sun beat down, a white plangency in utter blue skies, yet the heat did not oppress, for the Daluçan gods had raised freshening winds out of the propitious quadrant. Their great-winged god turned lazy gyres in the void above the masts and sails; and the other, much bigger and tailed like a fish, swam alongside the ship. She breached at intervals, white detonations going up when the god crashed over sideways rather than slipping splashlessly back into the sea. The Olorumi choirs had sung, the priest-dancers offered their benisons, and now the multitude was silent, except here and there where a beautiful young woman wept quietly. Aboard ship a smaller crowd looked back at the shore, and among those pale Daluçans were a darker few. New wives stood beside new husbands, and Aqib saw some youth too, grieving to leave his home, sobbing in fact, but comforted and murmured to in the burly arms of his Daluçan knight. Aqib's gaze flitted between that pair and his own soldier, alone at the gunwale with the bright green scarf tied about his neck, waving and waving, his features dimming already in the distance. Some girl on shore screamed a Daluçan name, and another woman, another Daluçan name. Behind Aqib's lips yet a third name fought to be wailed out.

Then a young woman broke from her mother's embrace and ran into the sea and she drowned. A second girl splashed into the waves but was wrestled to shore alive.

Aqib shouted. LucrioLucrioLucrioLucrioLucrioLucrio. The sea would surely bear *him* up, and he could race across the shining plain and catch up to the ship, and all would end well, nothing would be too late. Salt flooded his mouth and he came up with a hack and wheeze, but fought on toward the offing into which the ship had vanished. His sight and breath washed away, but blind and breathless he could still strive in the direction of love, or else die. For that too would be acceptable, to die. Some Saint's hand stretched from Heaven and plucked Aqib from the waves, by the hair wrenching his head upwards out-of-water. Even struggling with all his might Aqib was exactly nothing to the power of that Saint Who dragged him easily back to the shallows and threw him onto the beach. Trembling and facedown in sand, Aqib lay there vomiting water. He groveled and retched and coughed until he thought he must die after all. No Saint—it had been the Corporal, who kicked him in the side, shouting abuse, until Sister and Master Sadiqi drew him off. Aqib sobbed and wished to die.

Part Two

Therefore she understood that, more or less, no
one is guilty. Or more precisely, that the guilty
exist, but that they are also human beings, just
like their victims.

Joseph Brodsky

[*FIRST NIGHT*]

Lucrio subsided then, and let Aqib speak for them both.
"*Menials*—be assured the owner of this fondac, your
master, who's away at home but should, as you say, return
tomorrow morning, shall hear this stern address as well.
But let us reach some clarity, we who are here tonight,
concerning the dignities and comforts owed to one of the
Daluçan Embassy."

Aqib held forth upon such dignities and comforts, and
none save the girl in the green neckerchief, a by-blow of

the owner, clearly (as she seemed to fancy herself some species of manager), made so bold as to offer back what had always been standard practice at the fondac, in contrast to these very novel requirements.

Aqib clapped, startling everyone. "*No,*" he said sharply. "We'll have none of your lip, missy. And furthermore there shall be—" He paused, looking over the three gathered, who squatted on their haunches before him. "But where are the rest of you, the other menials who work in this fondac?"

"Royal Cousin," said the girl with the green kerchief, "some are in the kitchen cooking, others in the refectory, busy serving—"

Again they were astonished by a crack of handmade thunder: "*Fetch them.*"

Two cowered; the girl leapt up and ran, returning on the double with seven others wearing dingy kerchiefs, tied at head, arm, or neck, as drudges do.

"Now that I may address you all"—with a touch upon the arm, Aqib shushed Lucrio, who had made to speak—"Master Daluçan's rooms are not to be disturbed for any reason, at any time. He will have *no* attendant for morning ablutions, nor food brought in to break the fast. In this fondac, there shall be no spying—no gossiping—whatsoever. Nosy busybodies, creepers in the hallway outside the door, and curious eyes peering through windows: all these shall meet with *severe redress.*" Burned alive? Beheaded? Flung off a cliff into the sea? The gravity of Aqib's tone was such that no doom seemed too far-fetched. His gaze bleakly met each menial's in turn, so that none should lack for a moment to consider how fools may come to sorrow. "I trust I've made myself perfectly clear?" Heads nodded all around, and voices lifted up—

"Yes, Royal Cousin, oh yes!"

—unanimously. The smallest boy's eyes filled with tears, lips trembling. The twin girls clutched each other's hand. Aqib caught not one flash of rebellion or cheek anywhere. *Good.* "And we pray, too, that misbehavior on the part of *one* should not make *all* of you suffer. That would grieve us. You may go." The menials fled. *"Veni, Lucrio."* Aqib led his lover past the hanging carpet, into the room.

The dim glow of a night-lamp revealed the room's adequate appointments. Aqib begged to aid in the disarmourment, and so Lucrio explained the way of it to him. Their hands at opposite sides, they sprang the catches interlocking chest and back plate of Lucrio's cuirass, the tunic beneath all sweated-through. Now it was comfortable to embrace. "We'll not have to worry about *them* I shouldn't think," he said. "I put the fear into them properly."

"You put it in *me*," Lucrio said, and kissed him before speaking again. "Damn, though! That was *mean*, Aqib."

"It was necessary, I assure you." Aqib lifted his arms—the shirt pulled up and off him. "I cannot say how the menials are in Daluz, but here in Olorum one cannot permit them free rein. They are to be taken firmly in hand." Aqib's belt crashed to the mat-covered floor, his trousers falling, too. "Loose tongues and sly eyes, rumor and intrigue: many a household has been brought low by menials left masterless." Lucrio disrobed, and Aqib, wondering, played fingers down the valley between the deep halves of his lover's chest, there where soft dark hair grew thickest. "And now you and I share a secret that must be kept."

[*SECOND DAY*]

In the white sun-blast of morning, Aqib slaughtered an old lamed bongo at the Menagerie and threw its meat to the cats and dogs, while dwelling upon the night before, satisfied. Sometime while the long gold afternoon waned into red, during the nervy first free-flight of a fledgling hawk, he began to wonder what other things two men might do together when they lay down: more than gentle touches, more than soft kisses. Dusk had gone blue, not yet violet, and the menials were trudging in with emptied shitcarts, when some old memory came back to him *re* a poet he'd once heard declaiming near the port. That wild crowd! Its howling laughter! What lewd words *had* that poet spoken? And then, late night at the rendezvous, in black shadow and orange lamp-flicker, Aqib strung together the remembered words as best he could: "*Ego tibi fututrix. Volo crisare et cevere; tu me pedicare et irrumare vis?*"

At once Lucrio seized him close in a huge-handed assault. With violence, with possession, Aqib was kissed, bitten, a tongue thrust into his mouth. Then he was shoved back, half-crushed, to arm's length while Lucrio gaped at him. "You know what you just said?"

"No!" Aqib said, delighted. "Did I say it correctly, though?"

"More or less, but *Aqib*—!"

"I wanted to surprise you." Aqib stuck a hand in his lover's clout, and was gratified by discoveries. "It was awfully wicked, what I just said, wasn't it?"

Lucrio boggled at such understatement. "Yeah!" he said. "No, stop—I'll come too fast. Quit, Aqib! Where in the world you *heard* all that, anyway?"

"In the Low-Port market, when I was a boy. There was a poet reciting, and the crowd exclaimed at every verse.

They laughed and rolled on the ground. Then some king's men came and took the poet away. My father knocked me down when I asked him what the words meant. He'd never hit me before, nor has he since. May we now do those things I asked for? Tonight?"

"You don't even know what all you *said*!"

"Who cares? I want to do it all anyway. Whatever pleases you, Lucrio, will delight me—*please*?"

"Well . . ."

[*THIRTEENTH DAY*]

In the last days of the Daluçan Embassy, His Holiest Majesty's youngest and favorite child, the Blessèd Femysade, had returned home from university after years abroad in the north. Consumed with her studies, she never granted the Daluçans audience. Indeed days after they had gone, she still had not stepped from indoors the Sovereign House. At last, the Most High put his foot down. And so the Blest made safari in the Park with the king her father and many attendants. As she had been of age to marry for some years, His Holiest Majesty pressed her on the subject, which bored her, as did most men. Then, from afar, the royal host glimpsed Aqib running

Sabah. He rolled in the grass with the growling cat, his wild hair loose and gathering chaff and golden straw. He wrestled with Sabah, and laughed: joy nowhere and with no one else, now. The Blessèd Femysade recognized him at once. She turned to the king and said, "*Him,* Papa." With that, Femysade and Aqib were married even before the Long Rains fell that year, and their daughter, Lucretia, was born before the Rains fell again the year after.

[*THIRD DAY*]

At first light, Aqib sat up abruptly in bed. "Oh, Blood of the Saints," he exclaimed, "the bears!"

Lucrio propped himself up on an elbow. "Bears?"

"Well, you *can*not be imagining they teach themselves to dance."

"Never really thought about it." Lucrio lazily took in the view as Aqib crouched and stood, crouched and stood—naked—rummaging the floor-strewn clothing. "But, yeah, I could see that somebody's gotta learn 'em."

"Someone indeed," Aqib said grimly, wrapping his loins in one of the clouts. "Would you care to guess who?" Lucrio glanced at the other clout, opened his mouth to say something; closed it, and didn't. "And in three days' time," Aqib said, drawing on his shirt, "I'm meant to give a show for you all, the whole Daluçan Embassy. By then my bears had better be prancing winsomely, or so I was advised by a herald of His Holiest Majesty..." It occurred to Aqib that, first thing in the morning, one might better eschew complaints of ursine intransigence, and stick to tender talk. "But tell me, *mi mellite*," he said with a smile, looking up as he pulled on his trousers. "What do your Daluçan knights of the Tower require of you today?"

"They got me doing exercises all day long with one of your armies. Drilling your guys in *triplex acies.*"

"Oh," Aqib said, without a clue what the term might mean. "Well, that does sound like fun, I'm sure!"

Lucrio made a face. "Some boring-ass bullshit is what it is. I'd rather be laid up here with you."

Aqib, however, had a long day ahead too—with recalcitrant bears. They dressed and hastened to their work.

[*FOURTH DAY*]

Did a shadow cross the light? Aqib opened his eyes. At the bottom of the room, one third of the window-shutter was folded open upon the fondac's garden, admitting sun and birdsong. Last night, in hopes of some breeze to stir the room's steamy closeness, odorous of man and boy and their rutting, they'd dared risk an uncovered window. Now, blue tatters of sky in a green leafy frame could be seen, brightening. Lucrio breathed still sleeping against his shoulder; a huge arm across his chest, a thigh big as both of his lying over them, keeping him close, in place. Brisk steps went down the hallway, rustling the portiere in passing. Aqib closed his eyes to the faint noise of folk breaking their fast up front in the fondac's refectory. In a moment, they must rise and away: Lucrio to put the Olorumi Royal Cavalry through its paces, practicing whatever difficult formations, and Aqib to the Menagerie and its many chores. But for a little while longer, he could lay sleepily enjoying the weight of muscled limbs, the sweaty press of skin on skin, Lucrio's phallus hard against his leg, and pulsing.

[*FOURTEENTH DAY*]

The aunty-broker met with Berasade mln Sun Above The Fog, who signed without a quibble, for the opening bid came in stupendously lavish. Berasade took the news to her father, Master of Beasts and the Hunt, Sadiqi, who summoned in turn his elder son, styled "the Corporal." These three took conference. Sister and brother then brought the news to Aqib. They sat him down and laid out the details: the who, the when, the how much. Aqib listened quietly even as his siblings veered off into giddy speculation over their own much-brightened prospects. When finally they allowed him a word edgewise, Aqib said—hardly *knowing* what he was saying—that, having heretofore belonged only to the lay priesthood, he found himself seized by sudden vocation, and moved to take the fullest, strictest vows. He felt disposed now in his heart and soul to a renunciate's life, and wished only to wander skyclad and prayerful, for all his earthly days remaining—

—Starting in fright, Aqib lost the thread when the Corporal stood and struck the wall; but smoothly Aqib picked it up again, saying only, "Celibate . . . ," before the Corporal kicked the stool out from under him.

Women being weaker than men, they will often break at the sight of strength brutalizing helplessness. Aqib, then, knew whence salvation would come, if it came at all. Whichever way knocked, he always turned his eyes back to Sister. And she did soon rise from her own stool, saying, "Really, Brother," to the Corporal, "I do think that's quite enough. Must you *always* . . . ?"

The Corporal spun on her, spraying spit as he spoke. "You defend him? *You,* who are playing two royal grandsons and a royal nephew against each other? And how many other fools vie to make you the best bride's-price? I wonder, Sister, whether Olorum's best will still come sniffing around you, if *this one* spurns the king's favorite, spitting in the face of the Blessèd Femysade! Who will marry you, then? Or would you rather end up some, some—*merchant's wife*?"

Berasade recoiled. For that, most decidedly, was not a fate she wished for herself. Merchant's wife, indeed! Averting her gaze from brothers younger and older, Sister gathered up the layered hems of her skirts, light linens all richly colored. And speaking no further words, Berasade mln Sun Above The Fog withdrew—leaving them to it.

The wife had never lived on this earth more content and better pleased with her husband than would be the Blessèd Femysade, once she'd married the son of Sadiqi, Aqib. The world would say she *glowed*—warned the Corporal—they would say how happy the Blest seemed now, so changed, so full of joy. And *babies,* they would say. So many babies! One right after the other! Sweet Saints above, what *could* those two be doing . . . ?

[*FIFTH DAY*]

At that time, more than a generation had passed since the Kin-Slaughters, though elderly Cousins still remembered the terrors of early childhood, that bloody feast of fratricide, the rampant murders. Therefore, most great houses retained a few burly fellows who, wearing the clan livery and bearing battle spears, kept a beady eye on the coming-and-going of menials and grandees in and out of the compound of their liege. The Reverend Master Sadiqi, to be sure, was of the old school, and had guardsmen who watched at the house gate and in the front courtyard. Fortunately, vigilance and discipline were much fallen off after so many decades' peace, and nowadays, directly after prayers, the guards doused the lamps and went to bed. The way was left clear for a skulking boy to slip unseen from his father's compound, run down to the undercity, and fit himself in the arms of a forbidden lover.

Aqib, glorious and out-of-place—like blue glistering diamonds round a beggar's filthy neck—had eyes for no one in that late-night crowd as he passed through the fondac's bustling refectory . . . though a whole host of heads spun and took note of *him*, on his way to some room in the back. Before he could touch him, Lucrio woke and drew Aqib down into the sheets. The first kiss lasted until Aqib broke it with his news.

"They were saying—*everyone*, Lucrio!—'the bells ring, and we all gather to worship the Saints. But where is Aqib? We never see him at midnight prayers anymore. Does he go down to the undercity, I wonder, and see some doxy there? Has he taken up, these last few nights, with some low fast girl?' Lucrio, I laughed at them, I tried to put them off, but then Master Sadiqi my father came to me. At first he said nothing, only looking at me, and then he said, 'We will see you tonight, Aqib, at prayers, won't we?' Oh, what could I say, Lucrio? *My father!* I said, 'Yes, Papa. Of course.' Therefore I come to you so late tonight, and must so tomorrow and hereafter. I *am* sorry to make you wait, my love. But never despair of me; don't sleep . . ."

[*SIXTH DAY*]

Along that stretch of day neither fish nor fowl—no longer night, not yet the morning—he and Lucrio walked up the boulevard so that Sabah could stretch her legs awhile free of the Menagerie. Overcast blotted the stars. The moon had set. Night-lamps burned, godslights shone, only far and in-between. Deep shadow abounded on the boulevard, and nearly anywhere at all two young men could tarry for a kiss and grope, unseen. What did they talk about, and talk about, and talk about? Always talking in those first days of love! One hardly remembers what was said, only with whom and how it felt, the balmy promise of the air. Then, a little fat pig tried the wide road. Oh, it ran! Fleeter than one imagines a pig to be, it broke across the boulevard... but not *nearly* fleet enough. A godslight overhung a huge gate, and by that whiteblue radiance they saw coursing shadows embrace, then roll together on the ground. They heard a squeal, a scream, and next they knew, cat lay down with pig, her teeth in its throat. Sabah strangled the small thing dead.

"What are we going to do with *that,* Sabah? Have you not already eaten?" Aqib came to stand over her, scolding. "I brought no *gamebag*. We don't *need* it!"

Insouciant, the cat stood up from her murder, licking bloody chops.

Lucrio laughed.

A great tenement-compound loomed right there beside the boulevard. From its courtyard a sleepless woman emerged with three children: one at the breast, one a toddling skirt-clutcher, and one six years old or seven. "Racuhzin?" the matron called. "If you ain't gonna take that pig, mind if we do? Racuhzin?"

Aqib looked to Sabah, who'd gone to wander naughtily at the boulevard's far side, investigating the cover of tangled overgrowth from which the pig had broken. Negligently he waved *have at it* to the mother and children. "Sabah!" he called, and the cat came.

"Well, go on, boy. Get it!" said mother to the biggest of her children. Lucrio helped the small boy hoist and settle the bloody carcass across his shoulders. The mother, humbly amazed by this assistance, said, "Thank you, Mr. White Man."

"*Salve, Daluciane,*" Aqib corrected sharply. *"Tibi gratias ago."* The which the matron assayed in a garbled mumble, while backing away she repeated, "Racuhzin," ducking her head and person obeisantly low.

"You all take care now," Lucrio said; and the poor family, to him: "You too!"

Having gained some distance, the mother and her biggest child began to chatter excitedly together, the boy staggering under his burden. They made their way back into the tenement's courtyard.

Lucrio held his hand out to the cat. She licked it clean of pig's-blood. "How'd that lady know to call you that?" he asked.

"Hmm?"

"What she said. 'Royal Cousin.'"

Aqib said, "Oh," and having been told thus all his life, and so believing it, said, "We Cousins have a grace about us which the little people"—one hand patting down upon the air, as milords indicate the plebs—"know and recognize. A sacred glow."

Perhaps. But one could certainly point to more concrete clues.

In the first place, nine-tenths of Great Olorum walked in bare feet. Aqib went shod. And though the sandals he wore that night were only his knockabouts, still, note how intricately wrought they were, all aglint and agleam with bronze rivets and bucklery. His shirt and trousers—albeit work clothes, and stained—were bespoke confections of Sovereign House tailors, made of cotton so fine the poor never handled such stuff . . . except to pick and prepare it for their betters. Hair scissored short was suitable for all Olorumi, of any status, man or woman, high and low. None but Cousins might wear it long, however, and Aqib's was extraordinarily so. In quality of teeth and skin, bright or darkened whites of the eyes; lips pale from overwork and poor food, or lips rich and fully pink; also in the assured grace of the body's movements, or conversely, in its pained, halt diffidence: one could read past insults to health and ongoing privation. Or one could spot a scion of superaffluence, slumming in the undercity.

Lucrio said only, "Ah," in the tone of a man enlightened. They walked on.

[*24 YEARS OLD*]

Behind his wife's palace in the feral garden, where a length of chain attached to a tree-shaded expanse of wall, Aqib watched his daughter romp with a lion rescued earlier that season from an overmobbing pack of wild dogs. In rank weed and flowers, six-year-old Lucretia ran laughing. The lion, still adolescent—still clumsy, too, on that mangled right haunch—chased and bumbled. Aqib watched closely. She did well. Lucretia was obeying her papa, and with sharp tones, strong gestures, put paid to any hints of leonine overexuberance no sooner than these arose. Yet Aqib was still anxiously aware of the effect his own presence exerted here: arousing docility and scruple, somehow, in a beast truly having neither. A moment's inattention, and the sneaky monster might well *eat* a child . . .

The majordomo materialized in the open postern entry, shouting. "Most Sanctified Cousin, a royal herald has come to—!"

Whereat the announced, himself shouting, shoved past the older woman. "Royal Cousin Aqib? His Holiest Majesty requests and requires that—"

Aqib swept an imperious hand behind him, stilling the jostling and noise alike. "Lucretia," he called. "Come at once!"

The girl called back to him, "Yes, Papa," and came running, lion at her heels. Resurgent hostilities abated between majordomo and herald, the toothy, clawed approach quelling them. Aqib locked the latent maneater collar-to-chain, and the beast dropped its head thirstily to the water trough. Taking his daughter's hand, Aqib led them all inside, to the mudroom. "Now what is this?" he said.

The herald wasn't brisk but *rude*. "Two gods are just now come from the western bayou. They wait at the Sovereign House, in the Daluçan Garden as we speak: demanding to see you, the child, and the Blessèd Femysade *forthwith*."

Aqib protested. Two *gods*? Such august beings could want nothing with him or his daughter: neither of whom had the least to do with high politics, and as for " . . . the Blessèd Femysade, she only reviews numbers: Treasury Chair and Treaty Signatory are, respectively, her mother, Grace of Saints upon her, and sister—"

"*You*, Sanctified Cousin! the *child*! and your Blessèd *wife*!" said the herald, his trained and honeyed voice souring with nerves. "Now, where is the Blest? I must fetch her at once."

Father and daughter glanced at each other in alarm. One did not plague the Blessèd Femysade with *petty bullshit* while she was in chambers—not twice, one didn't.

Any interruption of her studies was *some petty bullshit.*

"My daughter and I shall attend upon the visitors without delay." This, Aqib conceded in the manner the herald so clearly required: without qualification. "But with the Blessèd Femysade"—his tone now becoming one of delicately proffered recommendation—"truly, it were best she be informed as evening comes on, *after* siesta: at such time the Blest should emerge from her mathematicon."

There was a tizzied screech, a fluttering of hands: no one might put off a herald of the Holiest King of Kings, Sovereign of Great Olorum, City and Nation: *no one*! So Aqib washed his hands of the matter. And—no, indeed!—they *mightn't* have a moment to throw on appropriate robes, nor freshen up, either. Aqib and Lucretia were packed into a wheeled sedan, the puller-men departing at a dead run, nearly, toward the precincts of the Sovereign House. Passing the mathematicon's open casement doors, they heard the second power in all Olorum roar scatological abuse. Aqib flinched. Kept sweet, the Blest loved her jokes; she was fun and only playfully foulmouthed. *Never* provoke her, though.

Outside the ramparts of the Sovereign House, crows fed upon the impaled remains of a cavalry captain, *pulchrissimus,* who had often sought to catch Aqib's eye, or corner him in shadows, at fêtes and functions. Some youth, seduced; his parents, enraged; and then a public impalement. The captain was no longer surpassingly handsome, needless to say: a few birds lifted, cawing irritably, when the sedan stilled and the passengers alighted; they hungrily fell back to with the flock, as Aqib and Lucretia entered the gates. Awaiting them in the atrium, the Blest his sister-in-law, the Most Holy, and Her Grace—thronged by courtiers—broke at once into noisy babble, all the while hustling father and daughter down vaulted hallways toward the Daluçan Garden. Distractedly answering the query that rang out loudest, Aqib said, "The Blest was at her studies when the herald arrived," and that won him a moment's stunned and knowing silence. His attention was largely elsewhere.

What had he, as a child, ever imagined the "sin of Daluz" to be, exactly? Probably it'd been a thing *beyond* his imagining, as doubtless the matter was for little Lucretia now. Saints forbid she give it any thought! Had Aqib ever, then? Had he never wondered why these men alone among sinners were impaled . . . *thusly* onto spears, to die slowly before the Sovereign House, in full view of all Olorum and the Saints? Well, maybe not: he had been a *very* stupid boy, after all. The cavalry captain had pursued Aqib with such sly charm, so sure of his ground, that a bit of common knowledge must surely circulate in certain circles. No villain, by any means, that poor dead fool had only been too … thirsty. Those heavy-lidded eyes had used to track one's position, progress, every movement at midnight prayers and parties, at formal court audiences and devotions; those full lips always ajar and tongue peeking—tongue licking—in carnal speculation. Ever caught alone, Aqib might well have given up exactly what was desired of him. But he himself wanted life, not horrible death; and so never could the handsome seducer find him where a tryst might be fixed for later, much less consummated on the spot.

In her own way, the Blessèd Femysade helped his resolve. Sometimes she still complained that the vows of marriage enjoined a woman three times to faith, and yet never once required likewise of the man: "I'd *kill* you," she liked to say tenderly, tangling fingers in his hair. He rather thought she would, too. Therefore Aqib kept always right where eyes could see, never just out of sight. He cast his gaze aside whenever another man's sought to catch his own. And if ever on the road at night, he went accompanied by many attendants, his wife's spies among them. Never once alone since, since …

The Daluçan Garden.

Topiary trees. Clipped grass. Shining white marble. The colonnade, polished to glaring reflectancy, squared the rich lawn of the peristyle. There, in the center, grew a shady grove of mevilla trees, the branches freighted with many dark fruit and a few, here and there, just blushing orange. Two gods sat under the trees. One stood up—not six but *seven* feet tall—and beckoned welcome to Aqib and Lucretia, inviting them into the shade, among the strewn pillows. With the same gesture, the god waved off the royal crowd. Father and daughter walked alone from the colonnade, out under white light and onto the green grass. Lucretia lagged, clutching his fingers tightly.

The gods?

They were better looking than any people you know. Both women, they were a full foot taller than even the Blessèd Femysade, who at six feet towered over Aqib. The gods' hair—wonderful to behold—was scissored and combed into rigorously perfect spheres. Oh, they were beautiful! The younger god smiled very patiently, as some mother will smile to say, "Yes, it is, isn't it," when her baby exclaims, "The sky is blue, Mama!" Well, what else would it be? Olorumi were brownskinned, and Cousins generally of the duskiest, richest color. The gods were much darker, of truly black complexion. Or not exactly: imagine the iridescence atop a natural pool of petraoleum, though the effect was never so blatant, but rather at the very borders of perception, subtlest of qualities. Their skin seemed faintly faceted. Now and again, a glimmering prismatic rill would trickle across a god's hand, down her cheek, or along a foot: over any flesh exposed to the sun. Aqib sat where the gods gestured. Lucretia would not.

The elder god sat down with them, and said, "We are pleased to meet you, Sanctified Cousin Aqib, and you, Blessèd Lucretia—your parents gave you a *Daluçan* name, how charming!—but where..." The god peered to the right and left, with polite theatricality. "... is *she*, Blessèd among Olorumi, your wife, Femysade?"

Aqib thought to lie discreetly; then, considering to whom he spoke, thought again. (It was said the gods could *smell* a lie!) "Your summons caught the Blessèd Femysade amidst deep studies," he said, "and engaged in work requiring her utmost concentration. But I do assure you: the Blest hastens in her endeavors even now, that she may obey your summons at the earliest moment"—*possible* was untrue, and *convenient* insulting—"practicable." Aqib was pleased with himself. He'd cleaved to truth, however technical the cleaving. The gods were trading a glance; did the younger one smirk? "On her behalf and mine, I bid you the Saints' welcome to Olorum, City and Nation," Aqib said. "And you, Daughter, will you not greet our visitors, too?" Lucretia would not: she would crawl into her father's lap and turn her face to his chest. "Come now, Lucretia; mind your manners. Lucretia! I *do* apologize to you both." Aqib was aware he should reprimand the child and force her to behave in a manner seemly for her age and station. Femysade certainly would have answered such antics with a slap. But he too was a little overwhelmed, and solace may be had in giving it. He patted a hand on her back, and Lucretia sucked her thumb like a much younger child. How *did* one address the gods, properly? Which honorific . . . ?

"You may call us by our names, Royal Cousin. We Ashëans are not so formal as you Olorumi. I am the prophet Adónane. This is my granddaughter, who is called, hmm, let us say 'Perfecta.' She's the greatest of our miracle workers, paramount among magi of the Ashëan Enclave."

Adónane and Perfecta wore long loose shifts, sleeveless and monochrome. The prophet wore crimson, the maga a brilliant shade of saffron; across their naked shoulders, twice-wrapping the tops of the arms, the gods wore shawls of the same fine linen, but fabulously embroidered. The brocade told stories in the stitched shape of gods and mortals, minarets and grass huts; here a rain of bright fire, there what must be white driven snow. The god Perfecta, silent this while, had slipped a smooth oblong of ceramic from her pocket, and she stared down at it. The god's eyes tracked, as did his wife's or daughter's when sitting before a codex.

Perfecta glanced up. "I wish you wouldn't think of us as gods," she said. "Rather call us, 'children of the Tower Ashê.' Or call us Ashëans. Once, Cousin, there *were* gods dwelling on the earth, and this planet was a sink of poison before they reformed it and made all good things grow. A little of their theogenetica persists among us purely bred Ashëans. But even so, we are as human as you, Cousin Aqib, and just a little longer lived. Indeed, we are kindred in truth, you and I. Did you know that your great-grandmother is sister to my grandmother here, Adónane?"

"Osorio, Most Blessèd by Saints?" Aqib sat straighter, looking around as if family-legend might momentarily step out of the colonnade. "Does she yet live? Is she here with you?"

"Ah, no . . . ," the younger god said, regretfully. "Osorio hasn't come with us here, nor is she, mmm, *alive,* in any sense you might understand. She is become a Discorporate Intelligence—"

The elder god, gently chiding: "Perfecta."

Causing the younger to abruptly sum up: "—your great-grandmother is dead now."

"I see," Aqib said coldly. Quite how the states of *alive* or *dead* might admit of ambiguity wasn't clear to him. That it did so for these seven-foot sublimities nipped his heart of any budding sense of kinship. No, he was *nothing* to do with these immortal giants.

Perfecta turned from Aqib to catch the eye of his daughter, peeking out in curiosity.

"Blessèd Child, sit up a moment and have a look above your papa's right ear. Try looking into his hair here"—Perfecta touched the side of her own head, an inch or two back from the temple—"and tell us what you see. Go on, child—you'll get a surprise."

Lucretia looked at him. Aqib shrugged, nodded.

Short hair or none was the mode at court, so Aqib would have long since shorn his off, except the Blessèd Femysade wished it kept wild and long as on the day they'd met. His daughter's fingers rooted in the bushy thickets round his right ear. "I can't *see* anything, Papa," she complained, but then said, " . . . oh!" Lucretia patted an excited hand on Aqib's shoulder. "Oh, Papa, you have one *too*! You have one long hair growing just the same as theirs: *blue*!" Except on the very crown of their heads, where a patch grew black as any mortal's, the gods' hair was all some celestial shade: the elder god's as pale as the blanched sky of morning, Perfecta's as bright as the noonday heavens.

"So you have hair like ours, Royal Cousin," said Perfecta, "and by blood of your great-grandmother, even some vestige of Ashê's power comes down to you. That little witch-gift mutation of yours. Or haven't you marked that beasts obey, and get along better with you, and with your father, than with all others?"

Aqib recoiled, though he *had* so marked. "It's only that I was raised working in the Menagerie." He made the gestures of a man putting something unwanted from him. "I grew up around all manner of animals," Aqib explained. "And so naturally I learned to know them and their ways." He stilled his hands and made himself smile politely. "There's no great wonder in that. No 'magic.'"

Perfecta gave him a long look. She held up a hand, index finger extended, and—mimicking astonishingly—the god warbled, chittered, trilled. After a moment, a little golden songbird fluttered down from the mevilla tree shading them. It lit on her finger. "Now, Royal Cousin, *you* call the bird."

Of course Aqib could do no such thing. He shook his head, his smile becoming strained, even a little supercilious. The gods were fallible after all, it seemed. "I do beg your pardon, Perfecta, that I should prove so unable." Aqib spoke in a clipped tone. "I wish that I could obey."

The god reached out her free hand and said, "Aqib bmg Sadiqi," lightly tapping his right temple, above his ear, "*Call the bird.*"

At her finger's touch, the world's richness and vividity doubled; it trebled and redoubled again. Aqib's perception expanded into a whole other dimension. Bees' buzzing, locust-chatter, the birds singing: no longer was this empty noise. It was lyric'd music, song with words. In a distant courtyard of the Sovereign House, a bitty lap-dog barked and barked. *Welcome home, I love you, Whee, Yay, Hurrah.* Aqib had always . . . guessed? some of this: now he knew. Now he heard it plain. The opposite of overwhelming, this fresh discernment gave him heart: heartening as sunlight striking down through a fogbound forest, heartening as for the traveler—all turned about and lost in trackless murk—to suddenly find the way before him bright and green and known.

Aqib sang to the bird perched on the god's finger. *Will you not come and visit?* The golden bird flew across to his own finger. *Hello there, strange fellow,* she sang. *You've a lovely song!* Aqib laughed and thanked the bird and dismissed her again to the free air.

"Oh, Master Aqib." Lucretia seized him round the neck in an embrace. "Papa, Papa, that was *marvelous.* I kindly beg you ask the gods to do it for *me!*"

Aqib looked at Perfecta, who smilingly reached to bestow another such gratuity, but this time hesitated and drew back her hand from the little girl. "We Ashëan pure-bloods are born to our gifts: 'congenital' we say, meaning they are fixed and unchanging. But with you witches the life you lead, it seems, may shape your gift. Lucretia, you are so young that yours is not yet formed." The god looked back to Aqib. "It was a simple matter to open your eyes, Sanctified Cousin. You had yourself been struggling to do so all your life. Your Blessèd daughter, however, stands at the forking of many roads. At such a junction, I think I'd better"—Perfecta glanced at the other god, her grandmother, who shook her head—"*not* fix her feet to any one road. Best leave the child untroubled, that she come into her own."

Aqib thought he understood, but Lucretia *certainly* did not. As his daughter had not done in years, she burst into noisy false tears. It was the first stage of working herself up to a proper fit. Just then, the name and arrival of her mother, Aqib's wife, "*The Blessèd Femysade!*" was heralded from the marble colonnade. At once, that announcement quenched Lucretia's kindling tantrum. The girl scrambled from Aqib's lap to sit beside him in the grass; no less upright and poised than the gods, than her father—or, indeed, than the Blessèd Femysade herself, who crossed the garden swiftly to her husband's side and sat down gracefully there. She cast one cool quick glance over her daughter. The girl sat up straighter.

Pricked by envy, Aqib noticed that his wife had stopped to dress. And quite possibly the Blest's star *outshone* the gods': she wore sumptuous silks, two arms' worth of red-gold bangles, and diamonds of state. Certainly no one could call her splendor any less. *Oh, what do you care,* Femysade had said to him on past occasion. *You're pretty enough in rags.* Which missed the point, Aqib felt. Right raiment lent one strength, while the flesh was only weak. "Blessèd among Olorumi," he murmured, inclining his head.

"Husband." The Blessèd Femysade laid a proprietary hand, ink-stained, on his knee. She turned to the visitors with so little awe, anyone would have sworn the gods called round *every* day from the western bayou. Glancing over their storied shawls and bright gowns, the Blest spoke simple greetings: "Archmage," to Perfecta, and to Adónane, "Prophet paramount." An interrupted genius clinging, still, to patience gives a particular sort of pained smile. "You have called us from our studies?"

"We'll come straight to the point, O Blest," the elder god said. "Having now examined your husband and daughter, we believe *you* are the one foretold to aid the Ashëan Enclave in its greatest enterprise. For such help as you, Blessèd Femysade, can give us, the Ashëan Enclave would remunerate you—and all Olorum, City and Nation—in coin, in goods, and in kind: with knowledge and miracles."

"Mm." The Blest smoothingly ran a hand over the folds of her gown. "And what boon does the Ashëan Enclave seek of *us*? Devolved and short-lived creature that we are."

The younger god looked up from her oblong piece. Aqib could see now that her ceramic flickered, tiny colored lights or images washing indecipherably across its surface. Grinning in triumph, the god Perfecta seemed not a moment older than her apparent age of twenty. "Nana, she's savant!" the younger god exclaimed joyfully to her elder. "The Blest has an *extraordinary* witch mutation!"

The elder god's face woke joyfully too. "Before going further, O Blest," Adónane said, "we'd like to ask a question meant to evaluate your eideticism and *savance*. May we?"

This unmistakably roused the Blessèd Femysade's interest. "Is it a test?"

Adónane nodded.

"Then certainly you may."

"Perfecta, ask her a three-body problem, and aloud, using no telepathy, nor the retinal laser, either. If the Blest can retain the whole unaided, without augmentatives, then *with* them she's guaranteed to be able to—"

"Nana, I *know*!" The younger god, staring at her ceramic piece again, said, "The bright medium is working on a problem now. And here it is: we Ashëans, O Blest, make use of microsingularities in our science, as models; and so we'll ask you to consider these in a straightforward three-body problem: smallest orbits smaller, both orbiting the third, largest: 2.145×10^{13} kg, 1.715×10^{15} kg, 5.71×10^{20} kg, respectively; diameter, for all three, .137 mm."

The Blest said, "Standard deviation and mean of orbital resonance?"

"Oh, please," the elder god interjected. "Never mind all *that* fuss! We'd just like to see some rough math hacked, that's all."

The Blessèd Femysade said, "So then you mean . . ." and spoke a long equation.

"Yes," the younger god said, "precisely. Time elapsed and starting position and velocity as follows . . ."

"I wonder," the Blessèd Femysade interrupted, "earthbound *singularities,* as models?"

"Do not be alarmed. We have means to contain their gravitational fields, although we cannot, unfortunately, prevent the gravities of the planet, moon, and sun from acting upon *them.*"

"That is unfortunate: complicating, one imagines, all your computations by many orders of magnitude, and compromising too, one would have to think, the ultimate predictive value of every modeling scenario."

"An ugly problem, yes." Perfecta sighed, with a little concordant nod. "One we should *so* like to turn over to you, soon. And it seems, O Blest, there's no need to bring you up to speed anywhere." The younger god Perfecta looked up from her hand-piece. "Shall I skip straight to the numbers then?"

"Yes," said the Blessèd Femysade, "do." She looked downward and aside, her gaze abstracted, the corners of her lips upturning in the slightest smile. (It was the countenance of a daydreamer, a cloudgatherer, some stranger might have supposed; but Aqib knew this attitude signified the opposite: the Blessèd Femysade's attention at most keen.)

"As though watching from singularity tellus," said the god Perfecta: "Singularity luna revolves at $3^h\,4^m\,33^s$, $17°\,11'\,55''$, with singularity sol at $15°\,1^h\,24^m\,41^s$, $8°\,53'\,57''$—"

"As though *you* were the watcher . . . ?" the Blessèd Femysade interrupted, murmuring dreamily.

"Yes," the god said, and returned to speaking the requisite quantities. As soon as Perfecta had finished, the Blessèd Femysade began to spill forth numeric babble, which after some time she broke to say—more apologetically than her wont—"The last few hundredths of a percent cannot, of course, be accounted for with certainty. I therefore finish with fatidic notation."

The younger god, who stared avidly into her little handheld ceramic, all achirp and aglimmer, glanced up. "Yes, of course," the god said. "Please do go on."

The Blessèd Femysade spoke, and finished.

"*Well*, child?" The elder god exclaimed to younger,

"What does the bright medium say?"

Ah, *interesting*—the gods too can suffer crushing disappointment. With trembling voice and clearly on the verge of tears, Perfecta said, "She cannot be the one, or else the prophecies are voided. The Blest has answered wrongly." The younger god spoke another, presumably differing and correct answer.

The Blessèd Femysade listened with head cocked at first in bemusement, then shaken impatiently. "Faulty numbers, maga. You fail to calculate observer effect—which condition, be reminded, you *did* require. Factor once more, this time including the perturbation you would cause as a telekinetic watcher. My assumption was that, as Ashëan archmage, you would minimally disturb the observation, and could approach pure quantum measurement, having attained pellucidity. Can you; have you?"

Perfecta sat a moment, lips parted, the question appearing to catch her up short. "*Of course,*" the god said as one whose honor is grossly impugned; but then, confessionally: "for the most part."

"Well, do not sit there mouth-hanging-open, child!" the elder god all but shouted. "Have the bright medium *recalculate.*"

"I am, Nana; I have!" Perfecta again watched her glowing ceramic. "And it appears that the Blessèd Femysade is . . ." *correct*! She was, verily, the subject and objective of the gods' long wait and search these many generations.

Why now? Why today? Aqib may have spoken the questions aloud.

Ancient auguries, refined only yesterday in a scriptomancy cast by Adónane, had brought the gods here today, to them. Lucretia, daring to speak up, said, "And please, O Prophet, with what question did you qualify the cosmogenetic probabilities?" though she couldn't've but known the price of such forwardness: mother reaching round father, and with fingertips, smiting the back of her head.

Adónane, indulgent, answered. "We knew from past great oracles that the Awaited One would be full grown at this time, living in some great nation. We knew too that she would very likely be a witch of strange mutation. *Who*, we didn't know, nor *where* exactly. So those were my questions, Blessèd child. A lesser prophet gives terribly vague answers, in obscure words; and in recent generations, the Enclave has given rise only to prophets of lesser gifts. Mine are not, however: and great power speaks with clarity. When I awoke from trance, this is what I'd written." She passed across a sheet of creamy paper. The Blessèd Femysade glanced, and then set it aside in the grass. Pensively she looked out into the glare-washed middle distance beyond the shady grove.

(Aqib gathered the paper up, but found no images thereon: only women's business, a chicken-dance of blots and scratches that yielded no meaning he could glean. He passed the sheet to his daughter. "Pumpkin? Will you make sense of this for your papa?"

Lucretia looked the scribbles over. Her father had whispered, so she did as well. "It's very easy, Master Aqib," the child said. "The paper only has our names, all squoze together without spaces. *LucretiaAqibFemysade* is written here."

"Thank you. And do say 'squeezed,' darling." He kissed the top of his daughter's head.)

They were very canny, Aqib thought, in their manner of persuading the Blessèd Femysade. The gods offered her nothing material. "Such capacity as now you have, Blest," said the elder god, "to grasp and parse a problem would be enhanced one thousandfold. Yes!—it *is* exciting, isn't it? At home in the Enclave, we have prosthetics that can magnify a superior mind even to that degree. With a flickering thought, you might disentangle seeming paradoxes that would cost you a lifetime's struggle in your mathematicon. We have such *wonders* to show you, Blest. Ashê's true gods left to us, flying in the uppermost airs around the planet, a sentinel eye trained out upon the universe. With it, we can see to the surface of other worlds, and watch the comets pass, even as closely as that bee there settles onto that flower. We Ashëans have means to step, a living ghost, from our bodies, and then *walk* upon those distant worlds, or ride those comets across the sky. And though you, descending impurely from Ashê, lack sufficient telekinesis to requantize matter, still, in our sanctum across the bayou, even a witch-miscegenate such as you can work miracles. And so many marvels besides, we hope to offer you, Blessèd Femysade: *knowledge.* Science of the highest order, all spread out at your feet . . ."

Her eyes shone. Never had Aqib seen the Blest quite so moved. Not when she'd sometimes allowed him into her mathematicon, in bygone days, to sit quietly watching while she worked, and then some rare *eureka!* lit up her face. Not after the best fêtes, sublime music, delirious dancing, heady wine. Not when trying his utmost to please her well, and doing so—or so said her softly relaxed body, her limbs sprawling out, smile lazy and affectionate. She'd said so in words, too, at times. And one could trust any praise the Blessèd Femysade offered, for she never gave too much. Aqib hadn't seen her look so when Her Grace the Queen took from the midwife's hands a whole and healthy infant, and settled granddaughter into daughter's arms.

She will leave us, Aqib thought. Then it seemed to him that, if the gods had already labored at this endeavor for so many of their long generations, then the Blest's help notwithstanding, a solution could hardly come overnight. The Blessèd Femysade might be away from him, from her daughter, from Olorum itself, for much longer than a season or two. It seemed to Aqib that years and decades—maybe all of a lifetime—were more likely. Tenderness *was* in her, and Aqib must appeal to it. He must beseech his wife to consider them, too, in her decision—

The younger god, with a fulsome smile, turned abruptly to Aqib. "Sanctified Cousin," said Perfecta, "I think you'd better take your daughter to relieve herself. The child *really* has to go. And you yourself have yet to break the fast. Your tongue is parched for water, and your belly rumbles for food. Why not help yourself to some refreshment? We and the Blessèd Femysade shall linger here for a while, talking."

But Aqib wished to stay and hear! "But I—"

The Blest lifted a forefinger. "Husband."

"Darling, come with your papa," Aqib said to his daughter. "Let's find you a privy, and then see about some nuncheon, too."

"You will," the god Perfecta said, "let His Holiest Majesty know all we've said here, won't you?" Like some gust of wind, these words struck Aqib a soft bodywide blow, hot on his skin as sunny brilliance. (At times the gods spoke without moving their lips or making any sound. And yet Aqib could still hear them, as from a distance, tinnily, as now:

"Perfecta," Adónane murmured reprovingly.

"Oh, it's just a *little* geas, Nana! So, he'll tell our story nicely.")

They left, the Blessèd Femysade's pretty husband and obedient daughter. His one glance back stirred some ancient recognition. Seeing his wife so statuesque, so darkly fine, side by side with the gods, Aqib thought she *did* look some kin to them, a sort of lesser scion. Did the Olorumi cousinry owe all their health and height, beauty and longevity, to dribs and drabs of Ashëan ancestry?

No sooner had father and daughter come indoors from the colonnade than it seemed half the court of Olorum pounced on them.

"Well?" The king seized Aqib by both arms and shook him once, hard. "What in six blue hells do they *want*?"

Lucretia had seen huge uncles, huge grandfather, and huge Cousins handle her little father often enough, and with just such casual roughness, that she no longer screamed and threw herself desperately into the fray. She hung her head in misery, upset for him. Aqib saw the girl's nurse there in the crowd, and with a sharp nod bade the woman to bear his daughter away.

"They say that you, Most Holy, wish to build a sturdy fort beside the sea, the better to defend Olorum against the corsairs who raid our coasts so often. In aid of its construction, the gods would offer their every device and talent. The power of the Ashëan Enclave, they say, could raise a citadel such as the world has never seen. The gods say, too, you foresee that Olorum, like an ever-growing creeper vine, will sprawl out in new districts as the decades pass—someday extending as far north as the Monkey forests, just as lately the City has spread down the eastern bayou to the sea. The gods say this worries you. If the municipal sewers and irrigation canals already fall short of present-day boundaries, how much worse shall things become latterly? But even as the gods did construct the original public works, so would they happily modernize the City—how and wheresoever Olorum require it, according to your judgements, Most Holy. They would gladly populate all the new waterways with their tonic flora and purifying fauna, so that every Olorumi, common or Cousin, remains free of the plagues that now decimate the outskirt shantytowns. Yet the gods beg you to see, Most Holy, that these feats must try even the resources of the Ashëan Enclave—that such gifts must come dear."

Although most women liked *men,* powerful and strapping, some few did prefer a slim, gorgeous effeminate. Obviously the king would never have chosen the latter for a son-in-law, but the Blessèd Femysade seemed content with her choice. His Holiest Majesty therefore loosed his grip, and even pinched and jerked at the shoulders of Aqib's mussed robe, straightening it. For a moment or two, the king stood by in pensive amazement, considering lifelong dreams suddenly attained. It was the Blest, Aqib's sister-in-law, who spoke the burning question.

"And what do they want in return, Brother-in-law?" she said. "Something from Femysade, it seems—but what, exactly?"

"What else?" Aqib gave a fatigued little wave. "Maths."

"Maths?" cried the king, waking from preoccupation. "What *kind* of maths?" One knew by the rise and crack of his voice that His Holiest Majesty felt it absurd, exchanging a bit of women's business for such weighty boons. "What earthly maths shall my little girl do for them that the gods cannot?"

Aqib raised placating hands. "Holiest of Olorumi, I swear I do not know. One god said the Blest inherits a quality they call *savance*. The other said, she has a freakish talent for 'psionic modeling,' for—what did they call it?—'coding in three dimensions and time.'"

"Oh, surely not, Son-in-law," said Her Grace. "Surely you have misunderstood, Aqib-sa! Those are *Ashëan* sciences, and we mortals lack faculties even to perceive, much less practice them."

"The gods, Your Grace, said they would admit the Blest into their deepest sanctum across the bayou. There, aided by 'numinal prosthetics,' they say she shall surpass even their best. The Blessèd Femysade will know and see such things as no one now can. The quarks and quanta. A world virtual, and of spirit. Psionics. Oh, I do not *know* what all!"

"Steady, Brother-in-law." The Blest his sister-in-law cupped Aqib's elbow with a comforting hand. "Steady, there. If this has thrown us all into disarray, how much more so for *you,* poor little Cousin Aqib, summoned here so abruptly, without forewarning?" She was a very gentle woman, of calming presence and sweet voice. "The gods believe that my sister can help them with the Photoassumption?"

Aqib nodded tiredly. Indeed, he *was* very hungry, and thirsty too. "Yes," he answered. "The elder god, the prophet Adónane, said no one alive, no one who has *yet* lived, can do more to aid the Ashëans in joining the formers-of-terra, the true gods, who are now in heaven. The Blessèd Femysade shall teach the gods to become light."

Part Three

"Dey would fight yuh all night long and next
day nobody couldn't tell you ever hit 'em. Dat's
de reason Ah done quit beatin' mah woman.
You can't make no mark on 'em at all. Lawd!
wouldn't Ah love tuh whip uh tender
woman ..."

Zora Neale Hurston

[EIGHTH DAY]

Softness pressed his lips, and grit, and bitter salts. In lamp-light and shadow, he opened his eyes to Lucrio—stinking of horses, grimy and sweat-soaked—kissing him. Aqib caught him round the neck and tried to draw him down to bed, but Lucrio wouldn't come. "I'm all nasty. Let go, man!" He pulled away and, laughing, stood.

Aqib sat up in the sheets. "No, come to bed. I was

waiting for you."

"You were sleeping is what." Lucrio unfastened back from breastplate. "Just wait here for me. I'll be right back." He shucked off his tunic, muddied with sweat and dust. The hair of his body lay in wet whorls across his chest and legs.

"We'll only go and wash up again, once you've had your way with me," Aqib said. "So you may as well have me now, as you are."

"Nah. Let me wash up first. Cavalry maneuvers *all damn day* with the prince—mayhebeBlessed—and that man had us on the field even after dark, with god-slights up. I was thinking about nothing but getting back here, going out back of the *taberna* to the bathing channel, to clean myself up for you." Lucrio unwound his loincloth.

"But, Lucrio, do wear a robe out this time," Aqib said. "You mustn't go about thus, displaying your glory to any and all. It's . . ." a thing menials and drudges do, going about naked ". . . *bad form* to pass through the fondac un-clothed for bathing, causing scandal. We Olorumi are not so free with our bodies as you Daluçans."

"You're free enough with the doors closed." Lucrio crawled over the sheets and—rank and soapy with sweat—pushed him flat to take a kiss. "But everybody will be just fine. It won't hurt 'em none to see a bit of *culus* and *mentula*. They all either got one or seen it before."

Before Aqib could admonish further, or catch hold of him properly, Lucrio had leapt from bed and ducked away through the portiere—and no doubt he'd tarry, for he swam like an eel and loved to do so. The naked slap of Lucrio's footsteps sounded down the passage and out the back of the fondac. Already Aqib missed him; but he missed sleep, too, and inexorably subsided down into the sheets again. Lately the interval between closing his eyes to predawn gray and snapping them open for morning blue had dwindled to nearly nothing. Even hale and in love, youth had its limits. He'd rest his eyes for just a moment . . .

Uproar erupted at the front of the fondac—down where the hall gave to the refectory. A girl shrilled, and another woman. Then men bellowed, struck, and were struck in turn. Startled awake, Aqib thought at first these were the sounds of bloody murder, but then the furor resolved in his ears as overwrought bickering among menials left unsupervised. He rose from the sheets and threw on a robe—meaning to rebuke the whole lot of menials in terms none of them should soon forget. Aqib swept aside the room's portiere, stepped out, saw:

All the late-night custom had quit the place. Gourd bowls and clay cups, overturned or shattered, littered the

floor around denuded tabletops. Spattering half the refectory's palmyra mats was the tipped-over communal
dish of long-cook-gravy and corn. A wailing boy—the
child who filled the cups—made tracks up the hallway,
dodging past Aqib. Screaming, the menial with the green
kerchief pushed herself up to standing against a wall: the
whole left of her face already swollen from some heavy
blow, her lower lip split. Aqib now recognized his own
name being shouted amidst the obstreperities, and the
word "*Where?*" He ran headlong toward the ruckus. The
Corporal dashed together heads of cook (come out the
kitchen, clearly) and bouncer (come in from the porch)
and flung away the two men, stunned and reeling. Before
the menial could hurl herself onto the monster again,
Aqib caught the girl in his arms, said into her ear, "Fetch
Master Daluçan at the bathing channel," and opened his
embrace toward the long hallway. He hurled *himself* onto
the monster.

Aqib never could fight, being a coward and weakling.
Since two or three years of age, when his brother was
seven or eight, Aqib would only crouch, cover his head,
and cry. But to rebuke one's inferiors with sharp words
was one thing, quite another to lay hands upon the help-
less. Aqib knew the despair of that extremity only too
well: what it meant to have no recourse except to yield,
and yet be met with violence anyway. So the abuse of me-

nials was unbearable to him. No other cause—certainly not his own—would make him lift up his voice and flail his arms uselessly. The Corporal knew well how to get a rise from his too-gentle brother; he called this "rousing your spirits." Many a menial woman and girl had been pinched and roughly grabbed, men and boys had their heads bounced against walls, just to inspire such an inept attack. Normally he would then laugh while applying a beating to his younger brother. But tonight the Corporal was angry.

He jerked Aqib about, rag-doll-style, laying in slaps and shouts. "Whore!" figured in that noise, and " . . . your Daluçan?" The Corporal's hand struck right then left cheek, stunningly—palm and back, palm and back, as the harder sort of man corrects his wife. Repeatedly the soft world burst against a world of hurt, and wouldn't it be just lovely to catch a glimpse of Lucrio about now, rushing this-way up the long hall? To him it would doubtless seem that older brother meant to kill his younger, though that wasn't so. The little things understood within a family are unaccountable to others. That Big Brother only means to teach the baby a proper lesson, as before when they were still very young, as always. That nothing edifies a fool so well as pain. That, for soft boys needing to grasp real men's ways, nothing served better than a beating.

He dropped Aqib, who fell bonelessly. Before Aqib quite gained the floor, the Corporal snatched him up again by a wrist, dangling, and punched him in the belly, then let go once more. Aqib caught a low table's edge and pulled himself up to sit on the brim, hunched-over. The Corporal bellowed questions the wildness of Aqib's sobs rendered inanswerable. And resenting this failure to reply, the Corporal drew back his hand, fingers clenching closed for the sequel. Oh, had they really passed the point of slaps, gone on to fists now? Things rarely got so far.

Someone—Saints be praised—*Lucrio* caught the fist and, with it, plucked the Corporal up off his feet, bearing him through the air, over the table, and headfirst against a wall. Which was only a woven-reed screen, and swung outward, spilling the Corporal into the flowers and shrubbery surrounding the refectory porch.

Blows to the belly were *worst*. Even a shallow breath hurt. The nausea, and ache of abused guts, always made Aqib hate himself and wish to die. What's the use, he thought; why go on? Wonderful to be touched, though—*mirabile sensu*—by a man who didn't hate him. He clung to Lucrio. Then shoved him away.

"*Look*"—Aqib panted, short of breath—"*out!*"

Through the fondac's doorway, the Corporal barreled in with his battle spear. *Never* before had things got so far as murder! Lucrio stomped a low table's edge, caught the thick wood square as it flipped upwards. He caught the spearpoint, too, embedded deeply in wood; and flung away the table. The Corporal lurched aside, trying to hold on to the shaft and jerk the point free. Lucrio leapt to close the distance. Rocked by a blow to the face, the Corporal abandoned the stuck spear. Fists flew. A scuffle followed too fast, too entangled to parse. At the upshot, Lucrio had twisted the Corporal's arm up behind his back, making him kneel, then screech and beg.

As breath returned, Aqib began shouting one thing over and over: "Don't *hurt* him!" A brilliant idea it was too. But to whom, Aqib, do you address yourself, exactly—to brother or to lover?

To whom it applies!

Lucrio looked up. Love visibly transformed him when their gazes met: from something furious and strange, to someone tried and true. He looked down again. "Usually I kill them who come at me with spears. But since you're his brother . . . Still, you'd better not try anything else, or I'm gonna break your arm *at least*. Probably worse. So think about it first, hear?" Lucrio let the Corporal go.

They'd all gathered back, the night-working menials, with the rabble thrilling to crises of the quality, just as they ever had done. Off the boulevard, two passersby gaped from the doorway, slack-jawed as imbeciles. Lover naked, brother wallowing on a filthy floor, himself snot-nosed and cheeks slimy with tears: Aqib swiped a sleeve across his face and rose up with resurrected arrogance. "You two"—he made his thunder-clap—"*away*. Or the next names called by the Reverend Master Flagellant shall be your own." The gawpers at the door fled. "You menials, clean up this mess." Aqib swirled a managerial hand. "Tell the owner he may send to the younger son of the Master of Beasts and the Hunt for recompense. I will make good all damages." Cups began to click, stacked-up; or to scrap and clatter, as shards were swept.

Wine and long-cook-gravy mucked the Corporal's fine robe, and for so enviably tall a man, he did look cut down to size now. Wheedlingly, he began to say, "Aqib . . ."

Who sliced a hand through the air. *Shush.* Previously Aqib had drawn such daggers of gesture only on menials. "Go home, Brother," he said, in a voice suddenly verging on tears. "You've attacked a Daluçan. For that, His Holiest Majesty should run you through and roast you alive. Go home now—go in peace—and your silence wins ours." Aqib glanced at Lucrio, who was shrugging on a robe given to him by the cheeky menial girl.

The Corporal looked at his battle spear swinging up vertical, some nine feet into the air, as menials righted the impaled table. Making to speak again—and shown his way by the haughtiest finger in all Great Olorum—he simply left.

The girl with the green kerchief untied it from about her neck. "You were *wonderful,* Master Daluçan!" She laid her bright cloth across Lucrio's palm. "This . . . it was a gift to me. It's far-west silk, and worth something."

Lucrio said, "Thank you, Senie." *He knew the menial's name!* "And it's really good silk, too. I could wear it on my head when I'm working in the sun." Lucrio smiled at her and said thank you again. A charmer, that one, who understood well how the emotions of the saved sometimes compel a sentimental gesture toward the savior . . .

Not that Aqib wouldn't have snatched the filthy rag away, and restored it to the girl with a rebuke for her impertinence, if only his brief flare-up of mettle and spirit hadn't gone all to ashes again. Shakily, Aqib groped for a joist or wall to keep him upright. His lips were trembling; he bit them.

Next to importune Lucrio were bouncer and cook. "Master Daluçan, sir. Could you maybe see what you could do with that spear there? We can't even budge it."

His robe's loose sleeves slid down forearms thick and sinewy, which bulged more thickly still, and the cloth tightened to a second skin across the broad, packed muscle of his shoulders and back, as Lucrio strained to draw the spear out of the table. Sleepily blinking his eyes, Aqib watched this virile spectacle and thought, *Sweet Saints, how I wish that glorious man were mine own lover for me alone to love.* The spearpoint jerked, shrieked in wood, and popped free. Then, chilled by shock, he realized his wish had already been granted! Aqib giggled. Threatening to buckle, his knees barely held. A sob escaped.

"Oh, you're worn out, ain't you?" said Lucrio—right there suddenly, beautifully *there*. He looked so worried! "You're just all shook up and tired..." His beard and brown eyes blurred as if under running water. "Aqib...?" Why did his voice sound so faraway? Arms bore Aqib up as he swooned.

He woke first. Tender and stiff, his face hurt worse than it doubtless looked. Brother had a knack for dealing pain out plentifully, but with nary a lip fattened, eye puffed or purpled, nor any blood let.

Picked out in dawn's pale light, a young man's clutter disposed itself through the narrow room: clothing heaped wherever fallen; unstoppered wine gourds, empty; a half-eaten dish Lucrio must have brought in last night, now hideously swarming with roaches. There were all manner of equipage and packs, various arms and martial impedimenta—who knew what all those things might be? Aqib's eyes fixed on his brother's spear propped upright against the wall beside another spear of the Daluçan style.

He sat up and found Lucrio's signet ring, a huge thing of tarnished silver and semiprecious stone, slipped loosely round his own thumb. Always before, Lucrio had blinked awake as soon as Aqib stirred, but not today.

Poor love, he was looking much too pale by daylight: white, indeed. In this good light, Lucrio ought to have looked tawny and tanned from the sun. This morning, his pallor was unwholesome, purple flesh encircling his eyes. Nor did he sleep so decorously as before. Mouth open, he drew breath with a stertorous burr, exhaling loudly.

This ugliness somehow served only to quicken Aqib's love—and watching Lucrio, caring so much for him, made it hard to breathe. There was pain in his chest like some beast clawing to be free. *Dear Lucrio,* he thought, *poor, poor love . . .* But enough already, enough. Get yourself to work, Aqib.

He slipped the signet ring from his thumb and left it in the sheets. He befouled the pot; availed himself of soapberries, the washwater urn, a cloth or two; and then dressed. Awkwardly Aqib hefted up his brother's spear and made away for that morning's chores at the Menagerie.

[**34 YEARS OLD**]

The foreman stood at the enclosure's edge while Aqib caught a hippo calf breaching out of its groaning mother. He waded from the muck, ducked his slimy arms into the bucket of soapy water held for him: "Yes?" he said. "Tell me." The foreman said that, upfront in the court-yard, the reconstructed gate lay finished and ready for raising into place. Oh, and too, Reverend Master—said the foreman—some Royal Cousin down from the Sovereign House had come calling. She was asking for the Master's daughter Lucretia, may all Saints bless her.

There, hesitantly, at the gap in the Menagerie's pal-isade, hovered some Royal Cousin he hardly knew—by face only. She looked far too soft, far too fine, amidst the ugly mess of axes and saws, wood chips and raw timber, all littered about the recumbent immensity of the new gate. Seeing him, the young lady called, "O Most Sancti-fied and Reverend Master of Beasts and the Hunt!" She waved, too, every finger of her little hand fatly bejeweled: "Good morning to you—*hello,* there!" The child picked her way into the courtyard, over the rubble of construc-tion, screaming minutely in punctuation of every stum-ble. Shadowing her came a liveried crone, holding up and over a banana-leaf parasol.

Aqib wanted no outsiders about, especially today, but

the girl offered him every assurance that she was a most excellent friend of Lucretia's, and even alluded to the feat of witchcraft to be performed this afternoon. She fell silent then, little chit of a Cousin, for Aqib had frowned in stern astonishment. So one's dear and only child, it seemed, might have a "most excellent friend" whom one had never met or heard of: some chic girl who chattered intimate family secrets that should hardly be whispered. Aqib waved the Cousin in—no sort of outdoorswoman, as Lucretia was, but a queen's-attendant. She said she was a linguist and translator (a delicate flower meant for the indoors, was what she was, in watered silks, and slippers suited better to marble floors, or polished wood, than to the dung and dust of the Menagerie. Impractical child!)

"Well," Aqib said, wiping wet hands on his grubby robe. "Lucretia left before dawn with the prince and his men. They meant to hunt duck mid-bayou. But, yes, the Blest is due back very soon. Are you quite certain, however, that she asked you *here,* now?"

"Oh, no, Sanctified Cousin; it was I who did beg the Blest to attend upon her miracle." The little Cousin huddled prettily in the shade of her parasolist. "Would it be a fearsome bother were I to wait here for her, just a while?"

Aqib sighed. How could one persist in beastliness before so much gentle courtesy? "Not a bother," he said; and was counseling the Cousin to stay upfront by the unrisen gate, never to wander off among the pens and cages, when at that moment a sparrow flew by overhead singing *She comes!* Aqib said, "Ah, the Blest comes now," and Lucretia arrived. At a run, bathed and redressed; though she *hadn't* dressed in more ladylike fashion, Aqib saw with a pang. Lucretia pulled up short, beginning to walk, when she saw the Cousin and her father. That stride—a lope, a prowl—belonged unmistakably to an athlete, a hunter.

Lucretia's shirtsleeves were rolled to the elbow, which left bare, of course, the old lion's-bite on her right forearm. The macabre work of those teeth, looking hardly just rinsed of gore, *did* leave one rather staggered and gutted—though Lucretia had taken the wound, and healed of it, many long years ago. Still, Aqib felt sure the pretty little Cousin must have seen that prodigiously mangled flesh before, and it struck him therefore ... *overdone,* the fuss and flurry she made over the scar. Lucretia, too, might have more decently worn those sleeves pulled down. The whole scene keenly recalled some other, very similar, but Aqib couldn't for the life of him think what.

Beside the exquisite courtier, the sight of his daughter fell on his eyes anew—as would the apparition of some stranger. Aqib was a little shocked. One day, a tiny girl, Lucretia had asked to wear a youth's shirt and trousers: far more practical clothes for working in the Menagerie than the layered gowns of a lady. Carelessly Aqib had allowed it. But now Lucretia was bigger than her father, a strapping sixteen-year-old, and seeing this first-order Cousin of the Blood sauntering about in boy-dress brought home to Aqib how poorly he'd done by his daughter, no mother to guide her, no wife to guide *him*.

Lucretia clapped her hands. Aqib and the others present jumped in startlement. "Up now, boys," she hollered, pointing laborers to either side of the aperture in the wall. "Let's get this gate hung!" The men hustled. Lucretia waved her father and the Cousin back a safe distance, though only the latter went.

"Now," said Aqib, "you *aren't* to overstrain yourself, Lucretia. You do, I hope, still recall that big rock, the boulder? Your nosebleeds—do you remember them, darling—your dreadful headaches, for all of a season? Lucretia? Are you quite listening to me? We can always have down a proper gang of brutes from the quarries, and *they* can hang the gate, so, really, you *mustn't*—"

"Master Aqib," Lucretia cried, and bodily shooed him back, "for love of All the Saints, I pray you will stop your fussing, Papa, *please!*" She went down upon a knee, and lay hands on a great timber of the gate. Staticky sensation bristled through Aqib's hair and over his scalp. The robe clung to him, prickling. Arrows, or a spear, went effortlessly and untouched wherever Lucretia wished them to, but she liked a good firm touch for these true burdens. The gate's timbers, crossed by thick teak boards, stirred, raising powder from the dusty courtyard. A hot metallic smell began to charge the air. And the gate's top half jerked from the ground—floating up to knee-height. Lucretia stood, hands still upon a beam. Folk gasped, a man grunting in astonishment, some woman calling upon the Saints' succor.

Aqib looked about and saw menials peeking out everywhere from various corners and hidey-holes—though they'd all been *told* to make themselves scarce. Angrily he began to clap and shout.

"Oh, Papa, *really*. What difference can it make?" Lucretia called to him. "By now, all our people have surely seen me at it. And the whole world knows the prince calls me his 'Right-Hand Witch.'"

So Aqib stood down. He decided upon sharper words later on, and the crowd crept out to watch the feat. This wasn't one of Lucretia's wonted "miracles"—hurling some missile with great force and deadly accuracy—and she had once, when younger and more foolhardy, done herself grievous injury trying to shift a weight beyond her strength. Aqib cursed himself for the weakest of fathers. To be talked into folly, even *knowing* better! He clenched hands in his robe.

The gate rose slowly. Lucretia spoke no more. She set

her face. When seeking to shift terrible weight, from forehead to feet her body displayed its strength, muscle and tendons popping out in sharp relief, gnarling the surface of her skin. The gate rose further still. Lucretia perspired, her rigid face flattened to a mask of utmost effort. Nearly there, the gate rose.

Wonder held them all dumbstruck. In trembling commiseration, they leaned forward. Sweat purpled the back of Lucretia's fresh blue shirt.

Aqib roared. *"Now."*

Laborers swarmed up the ladders—slamming home heavy bolts, fastening the lashings into place—but for all this dispatch, Aqib cursed them coarsely as the Blessèd Femysade might have done. Moments passed, but seemed slow eternities. Lucretia went down upon one knee, not smoothly or by choice, but buckling violently, as if struck a blow. Indeed blood spurted from her left nostril, and began to dribble down her lips and chin, soddening her shirt collar. Aqib cried out in alarm, and so did the pretty Cousin. About to speak some grim covenant, Aqib drew in breath—oh, they would *know,* these laborers, the shit-ass malingering oafs, what doom awaited should his only child, the Blessèd Lucretia, come to harm!—and at last the call came down. "That's got it, Master Aqib!" the foreman shouted desperately from his ladder. *"Please,* Master—tell the Blest to let the gate go.

It's good and fast in place, now!" The hum, crackle, and stink of lightning left the air.

Aqib lunged. But the pretty Cousin reached Lucretia first—who was afoot already, and laughing even as she gasped.

"Oh, be *still*, you," said the Cousin, dabbing at Lucretia's nose with her sleeve. "Be still, I say. How you *frightened* us!" She pressed some bunched-up cloth to Lucretia's face, heedless of her precious silks. The bleeding staunched, and anyone could see Lucretia was well, but Aqib needed to stow his fear for her *somewhere*. He began to scold, promising nevermore for such, such ... "futile pranks," he called them. Amidst this fuss and to-do, a huge white bird—a seagull—came to ground beside the trio, crying out its savage cries. Icy dread washed over Aqib, but he dampened his panic quickly to more sensible emotion: sobriety and foreboding. *When?* he asked in return. The bird cried *quork!* and flapped up clumsily from the earth. Again in its proper element, the seagull vanished with swift grace into the void.

The girls stared at him, the witch of most renown in Olorum.

"Papa, what is it?" Lucretia spoke no longer with any hint of adult command, but as might a little girl. "What did the bird say?"

As he'd schooled his heart, so Aqib schooled his face

from bleakness. "Your Blessèd mother will visit us today," he said: "Just at the red hour, as afternoon divides into dusk." He saw the shock seize his daughter's face.

Lucretia took the elbow of the pretty little Cousin and drew her aside for a private word. The young lady nodded seriously to all Lucretia said, seemed to extract some promise in return, and then, sweetly shaded—workmen pulling open the newly hung gate for them—left under the shadow of her parasolist.

Lucretia wanted to rush home to the Blessèd Femysade's palace.

"It's hours yet, child," Aqib said to her. "We can hardly be late."

"Papa . . . !" Lucretia dashed on ahead.

He followed, *wishing* she wouldn't get so excited. He wished *he* wouldn't. Hope made the letdown worse. In the resolved quiet of the heart it was possible to say, "Give up; it's done," but in practice, hopelessness was too bitter wine for drinking day after day. One would steal a little sip of sweetness and wonder, "What if . . . ?" At which point no time at all would seem to pass before—again, already—one was tippling nothing but the headiest stuff, cup after cup of hope, heart leaping at the least little sign, as if this were some fresh new lesson, without years of broken hearts and a sea of tears behind it. Whatever melancholy words Aqib spoke to others, he secretly hoped the Blest might return across the bayou one day, and they would be friends again—most excellent friends—as they had been in the first few years of marriage.

His menials brought fruit to him. He ate. The menials drew a bath, and he wallowed awhile in cool water. They closed the shutters; he lay down for siesta. When his eyes opened, he rose and the menials had laid out for him, not morning cotton, nor evening linen, but formal imported black silks. He went to join his daughter in the mathematicon.

Tawny light streamed through the glass of the casements, the top half of one door thrown open to birdsong in the garden. The slate floor, etched over entirely with sigils and formulae, remained unchanged. The long stone table, however, was no longer monstrously cluttered. Just a codex or two—Lucretia's—lay lonely on a single shelf, though once codices had packed the shelves from floor to ceiling on three walls. By the table, his daughter sat on her mother's stool. She too had dressed in a nobleman's formal robes—hers colored womanly, a deep, drenched shade of blue.

At the table, Lucretia leaned on an elbow, hand propping chin, and started from deep thought when Aqib shut the door behind him. Blinking, she looked up and said, "Papa . . . ?" when in the middle of the floor, the

Blessèd Femysade appeared.

Father and daughter gave a little cry. They always did.

She seemed wholly present, *there,* in the flesh. But Aqib knew this for an image, and that he shouldn't attempt to touch. His hand would only enter the facsimile and vanish from sight, yet feel nothing of what was seen, as when one dips a hand into some bright reflection floating on the water.

"Sit here with me, you two," said the Blessèd Femysade. "On the floor." As she waved, Aqib and Lucretia took the indicated pillows at either side.

The Blessèd Femysade had only some dozen years on him, but those twelve years looked thrice as many now. She'd grown bony and frail, with her gray hair blanching white from the rigors of strange disciplines that empowered the mind to the body's detriment. She swam inside her Ashëan gown, huddling as if chilled under a heavy, rich brocade shawl.

Fret her not—the Blessèd Femysade would have no chatter, no tears. When she'd spoken her piece, a gaunt hand would gesture first to daughter and next to husband (or other way around) and then some few measured words were permitted.

"We had thought," she said, "to wait until the last days of my mortality, by such time as I would have learned and mastered more; but it appears that cerebral capacity in the short-lived declines precipitously as we age: so it is best to fix us in Discorporation, we mortals, at the mature prime of life, which I am swiftly leaving."

If one's wife is in the room, but one does not touch her, it may seem the truth of her existence is chiefly known by way of vision—*seeing* her there. But, no. In fact her body releases dim heat, and one feels that. Zephyrs rise whenever she gestures, and her gown rustles with each movement, and some moist warm air brushes one's cheek as she speaks. The sound of her breathing comes faintly to one's ears. And though the nearest thing to inaudible, still subtly reassuring, the throb of her living heart can be heard. How eerie, then, that all this was absent with the hollow grammy.

She gave Aqib a little sign. He drew breath, and hesitated. The Blessèd Femysade did not care to have the wrong thing said, or any of her difficult argot misspoken. She could be so frighteningly short-tempered these days, it was hard to remember her as ever laughing, kind, patient with him.

"Will you still be able to visit us?" he asked her; then hurriedly: "not as yourself, of course, not in the flesh I mean, but as a ghost—I beg your pardon!—I mean to say, as a Discorporate Intelligence? Like this hollow grammy?" The Blest sighed, as when Aqib was being especially stupid.

"Say 'hologram,' Papa."

"Like this hologram?"

"Have I not already made plain to you, husband, how very few children of Ashê, even pedigree exemplars of the genotype, retain the aetheric adaptation to self-cohere when Discorporate? Be assured that I, little mortal witch that I am, lie well outside the selection co-efficient. Post-mortem, the bounds of the *purissime* will almost entirely delimit my actions."

Tentatively, as one feels a way through thorny thickets, Aqib asked, "Does that mean . . . very rarely? That we shall see you perhaps not every year, now?"

But Aqib had exhausted her patience. The Blest answered with flat crispness. "My Discorporation will remain stable into the proximate psionosphere: therefore onieric communion is not out of the question, but neither to be looked for, as I shall be much-engaged and, at no time, perceptible to gross human sensoria."

Not a word of that understood, *none*. Aqib looked helplessly to his daughter—finding her crying in the softest possible way. His own eyes began to sting. "No, Papa." Lucretia shook her head. "The Blessèd Femysade means no." And Lucretia would know, for Aqib had very conscientiously sent his daughter to study feminine arts with the ladies of the Sovereign House. By now she could spit at you all manner of womanish this-and-that.

"I wish you both would be mindful of the extraordinary and unprecedented honor my Discorporation represents. Rarely do the Ashëans concede true immortality even to the best of their own. *Never* before have they allowed one of the short-lived to Discorporate. Now, the continuance of my work need not be tied to this body's survival"—no longer weeping so softly, Lucretia made a quickly stifled noise. "And you, girl!—your father, yes—but *you*, Lucretia, I would have expected to behave in a more seemly and reasonable manner."

"Mama," Lucretia said, "I only wish that I could see you one more time before you die."

"You are seeing me *now*. Talk sense, child."

"I mean, to embrace you, Mama. That you were *here*—"

"Enough, Lucretia!" The hologram of the Blessèd Femysade chopped its hand downward on the bias. "My one charge to you was to make no assault upon the equanimity necessary for a savant to avail herself of the numinals and cerebrics. You know very well—both of you—that emotionalism is contraindicated for the attainment of *mens altissima*. Yet still you attack my equilibrium with histrionics! If there is time before the Discorporation, I shall come to you perhaps once more, and then we may speak a little again: only supposing I find you both in better mind. *These tears!* For now . . ." The image vanished.

Neither as hologram nor otherwise did they ever see the Blessèd Femysade again. Much too small to hold her properly—when had Lucretia got so *big*?—Aqib nonetheless held his daughter as best he could while sobs wracked her.

What had the memory of his portly, lovely wife to do with this cruel, starved creature Femysade had become? Nothing about the latter recalled the former. During siesta, she'd used to lie naked with Aqib in the sheets, and they would kick their feet together, talking lazily . . . but those moments were many years gone. Such sweetness wouldn't come again.

Who could forget the scandal they'd raised in the Sovereign House, early on—going round always arm in arm, heads leaning together and whispering like dear close friends, as women do together, or men with one another? The whole court, shocked, had supposed they must be lying down only as sisters do, giggling into the small hours, and telling stories to each other at siesta, but hardly doing such things as could conceive a child: right up until Lucretia began to swell her mother's belly. And though Aqib had only wanted to make love very rarely, and then would turn to his wife ravenous for her, the Blessèd Femysade had never minded either the hunger or the wait. Had he cared for her? Certainly he had! But all that was done now. It was put away for good. Aqib could love no one who hurt his daughter so much. An untimely thought invaded his reverie. Suppose—

Just suppose, down some distant forking of life's road, on a much more joyful path than this, Aqib-who'd-chosen-differently lay beside Lucrio, who would have skipped the afternoon session at Senate only to lie abed with him, chatting intimately, both of them sweaty in the aftermath of love. Did all possibilities include that one too, somewhere?

Lucretia, catching her breath, managed to speak between hitches and gasps. "But you, Papa," she said, "I only wish *you* wouldn't always be so alone. You're not an old man yet—not at all—and neither king nor Cousins would fault you for taking a lover. Why not find yourself some woman to . . . ?"

He let her go and crossed to the half-open casement door. "Master Aqib?" Lucretia said, startled by this abruptness. He ignored her. The sun westered in a red course through clouds over the bayou's far shore, where the gods lived and Femysade would die. Sultry and indifferent, the evening was gathering. Aqib closed his eyes.

A thousand birds, each one a soloist, sang the vespers to him, and backing the birds another choir of one billion: the dry season cicada. Below in the courtyard, a boy—his nephew—threw a stick, and a puppy barked as she went bounding after it. Above in the vault, a silver falcon plunged toward earth, shrieking pre-victory. Aqib was privy to all this secret music, and even his most dogged, irresolvable anguish flagged and fell away in the face of the world's raw beauty. His teeth let go of his bitten lip. His aching hands eased their grip on the sill, no longer clenched so hard lest he tremble. Or wail. He opened his eyes and a few wet blinks sufficed to clear away the blurriness. This could be borne and he would bear it. Aqib drew a long shuddering breath. Life had some worth and meaning. It truly did.

[*NINTH DAY*]

At midday the Corporal would go up to the Sovereign House garrison and take his meal at the refectory there, among the champions, the warriors, the *men*. Most days, Aqib would have his tiffin brought down to him from home, and would sit in the shady quarter of the Menagerie's sunny front court, and often take his siesta there too, among the menials.

He'd winkled out the tiniest tin of gravy from his tray, and was happily pouring it over the biggest tin, though still quite small, of corn, when the pale shade darkened all of a sudden. He looked up, and sharply back down, in dread. The Corporal loomed over him, then sat.

"Aqib-sa," said his brother, not in the usual tones. Startled, Aqib looked over: the Corporal was smiling, his tone wistfully affectionate. "I wonder, baby brother," he said, "whether you remember that day we first took you down to the sea . . . ?" And the Corporal began to give a vivid résumé.

Of course Aqib remembered that day! He could remember nothing much *before* that day, the ocean, and his brother. Diversely blue, those waters had been so much vaster than the ones he'd known theretofore in the tub where Nurse bathed him, and the waters had needed no hand to smack them before making white splashes. The sea shallows were transparent, the depths aqua and turquoise, and distances very dark, like dusk in the east or western dawn. Foam lapped shyly toward his toes, but always demurred and withdrew without wetting them. So Aqib came down closer. He squatted to taste. How *foul* it was! And waves came back swamping over him, the carnivorous waters dragging him off hungrily. He screamed, and Brother—just as one prays in extremity that the Saints shall do—came and bore him up aloft, to safety. Aqib clung to his brother's neck, bawling. Papa said, "Give me the baby," and Sister said, No, to *her*. But Aqib wouldn't let go. He wanted Brother. *Taqiri* was the savior, *Taqiri* the one who had been there. All this while, Brother was patting Aqib's back. "Oh, you're all right now, aren't you?" He kissed Aqib's cheek. "I've got you, haven't I?" Saying such kind things, his brother had walked them higher onto golden sand.

Rapt, his dinner forgotten, Aqib listened. He hugged himself and looked down. Smiling, he felt his mood warm with deep fraternity, eternal forgiveness.

Such moments of perfect goodness had come again, now and then, over the years while he grew up. At times his brother was so kind Aqib glimpsed the contours of a different childhood altogether: happier and shown the way, with a best friend and ally, his brother as the wise one who'd already blazed a trail from baby to boyhood to man, and knew all the hidden pitfalls, and knew the safe way through. Aqib never did, though, hit on a way to . . . *earn* that better brother. If pure good fortune sometimes brought him, Aqib's own many failings inevitably drove him off. You wouldn't think torment and salvation could reside in a single figure.

"So, Aqib-sa, what becomes of the family without you?" the Corporal said gently. "If the king calls Master Sadiqi friend, even so, Papa's star at court is much come down since he married our Sainted mother. And, me—you know I must go north and fight on the plains, or else never make a name for myself. But they'll never raise a fourth-order Cousin to high captain, and never give me the command of one of those plains-forts, unless you thicken our blood. I need you, and Sister needs you, and Papa does too. Don't you remember when . . . ?"

. . . another tale from better days. The sweetest sort of grace came over the Corporal on rare occasions, and at such times they were able to be friends, he and his brother. They were *close*. Aqib hardly suffered hunger pangs in comparison to more red-blooded men, but a warrior could not be skimping his victuals, if he wanted to keep up his stamina and strength. Therefore Aqib passed over his dinner to his brother, who fell on it. The Corporal sat with Aqib there in the Menagerie's shade, companionably among the menials, and they both took siesta there too, curled up on a blanket in the grass.

The mood lingered when they awoke. And so they went out walking together through the boulevards and byways of Olorum—walking prodigiously far, too, even to the River's bank, and down the eastern bayou shore. They talked freely all the while, as they hadn't in years, or perhaps never before.

Seaside and after dark, among the shanties of the southwestern undercity, they stopped for supper at some tumbledown fondac made of driftwood and palm fronds. The back porch was only a few strides across pale sand to the dark waves, moonwashed and musical. And there wasn't meat in the long-cook-gravy brought out to them, neither pork nor buffalo, but pink langoustine and flaking fish: delicious. Afterwards, Brother put them on a wagon going back northeast, home to the overcity, for a little rest before prayers. Jounced on the crowded wagon, in the vinegar musk of workers' sweat, the Corporal told Aqib that, just two days back, His Holiest Majesty's favorite child had come home from abroad. And so, to celebrate the advent of the Blessèd Femysade, the king had called High Prayer: for men and women to worship together tonight. It would fall to the men's lay priesthood to dance the benediction. "Won't you stand with your fellows tonight?" asked the Corporal. "*How* you dance, Brother! There's such an anointing to it."

Aqib hesitated. He rarely danced anymore at prayers. Lay priests wore a thin white shift, which strenuous dance soaked to nothingness, such that the fine fit bodies (his own among them) stood entirely revealed ... In that sweaty crush of dancers—lifting, being lifted—Aqib had begun to doubt whether his thoughts were quite, at all times, where they should be. Lately when they called on him to take part, he'd begged off. And yet, the forbidden no longer stalked him from all quarters. To have surrendered singularly and in full, it seemed, meant he could be safe on other fronts. Only one man could sway him now. So Aqib said, "All right, I *will* dance tonight." After rest, he put on a lay priest's shift beneath his robe.

Midnight bells rang as they hastened to the Sovereign House. Orange lamplight spilled through frets of the carved wood doors, and everyone was afoot, clapping and stamping; the women singing, tonight. He followed his father and brother into the north of the prayer hall, those rich, high voices on the south just finishing the Call-to-Worship. Disloyally to his sex, Aqib much preferred a woman's voice in song. The Cousins seated in the north wore black vestments, every one. There were only bright gowns to the partition's south, weltering colors according to the arcane praxes of women. Brother found them space to put down their prayer mats. The Call ended. The cousinry sat. In the moment before prayers began, he heard the Corporal murmur an answer: "Yes, my baby brother *will* dance tonight," and Aqib looked down at his hands, smiling, when men smacked his back and shoulders. Soon a southern murmur arose beyond the fretted partition, as news spread also to the women. And prayers began. Cousins kneeling toward the east, the deep and light voices joined in unison chant,

A Taste of Honey

men from memory, women (who couldn't hold so much Recitature in smaller minds) using the crutch of paper, of literacy. His Holiest Majesty led them through a full lay of the Canon. When the king gave the sign, drummers began to beat benedictory rhythms and Aqib cast off his robe. He went upfront to the chancel with the other lay priests. It felt *so good* to do one thing well! How *wonderful* to feel oneself approved of . . .

Two of the men and another boy were better dancers than Aqib: crisper in their movements, executing stance and step with a clarity Aqib couldn't match. One man, particularly, was mighty in the turns and jumps. It was nothing for that one to add twice the power of the others to the basic steps, his handstands one-handed, his cartwheels full flips. Though these three Cousins were clearly better dancers, everyone preferred Aqib. Sainted drums were *man,* or so the Olorumi said, while Sainted dance was *woman.* One mounted the other, latter submitting to former; and therefore in the dancing of certain women, one saw self-abandonment to the Saints man or boy could never match. The female might give herself up to Saintliness with a holy passion nothing to do with pure technique or raw strength. A sacred thing, and seeing it, the congregation would cry out, "The Saints are coming down! Bring Them—dance, *dance!*" Such anointment fell only to a few women, to a couple rare girls . . . and to

Aqib. The aunty-brokers of marriage rated him so highly only half for his pretty face and manner. The other half owed to this: what the southern Cousins saw whenever worship mingled at High Prayer, and it was men's turn to dance the benediction, and Aqib danced among them—never best, but brightest.

Cups of water, sips of spirits infused with potent herbs, were held to his lips and tipped in. And once the drums began they never did stop, that Aqib knew of. Rapture grasps one thing fully and discards the rest. There was just dance for him. The next morning, he woke in his father's house, in his own bed: to the whispering of his chamber attendant. Here are bush tea and the fruits you like to eat, Young Master. Here is water for bathing, and a clean shirt and trousers to wear. Will the Young Master have something for his head, if it's paining him?

Aqib sat up, panicked. *Lucrio!*

He said, "Fetch a house runner," and slapped aside the solicitous hands. The runner was dispatched to speak a message in such terse, obscure terms no one might understand but the man meant to. (Regretting the night before, promising the one to come.) Aqib groped the breakfast tray while his other hand sought to block the rising sun. His fingertips found a little bundle of leaves and pinched it up. Sour freshness rinsed his foul breath away, scrubbed his coated tongue. Light became light, not daggers in his eyes. The pounding of his head calmed.

[*TENTH DAY,* MORNING]

Near noon, Aqib fed the bears properly with groundnuts and greens. Then he spoiled them with some honeycomb, dearly bought off a ragged bush-forager, who came by the Menagerie to hock choice scavengeries whenever short the coins a drunkard needed. The sister bears gobbled up each her half of honeycomb—the greedy guts!—and then each sister wanted a hand from which to lick away all the sticky leftovers. Aqib held out his palms. Tropical sun had faded the bears' rich color to pinkish at muzzle, crown, and a wide swath all down their backs from neck to stubby tail. Otherwise their short coats were deeply russet. Now the rigors of training were behind them, and the performance done, the bears' nervous appetite and sad reluctance again became a desire only for play—and to eat. Aqib giggled, the coarse tongues tickling his fingers. The fence creaked as someone leaned against it. Aqib glanced over his shoulder and saw a vision. He blinked and stared: but the vision stood there still. Lucrio had appeared at the boundary of the bears' enclosure.

Oh yes, of course—he must have entered the Menagerie by the secret way.

"That was *nice*," Lucrio called from the fence, "the way you got your bears up and dancing the other day." His hair clipped and beard trimmed, since the night before last; Lucrio wore the full battle dress of a tricenturion, only the plumed helmet lacking. "With just some talk, and waving your hand a little. I liked that a lot! All the bears I seen dance back home, in Terra-de-Luce, what they do is jam some iron up the bear's nose, then put a chain on it. Just a-pulling and a-yanking: that's how they make those poor bears stand up and dance."

"No, no, *no*," Aqib said, aghast. "Oh, I could never treat my ladies that way! We parley, we practice—I give them *treats*." Aqib crouched and roughly scratched a bear's side; she lay down and writhed ecstatically. "Though our bears of Summer aren't, I'm sad to say, the most fearsomely *clever* creatures. The bears of this continent do seem rather stupid, I'm afraid. Do you know—when I was just a boy—one of your countrymen came to Olorum with a bear from the Lands of Winter? Such a big, brown, lovely fellow that was! The handler and his bear gave a grand performance at the Sovereign House (and His Holiest Majesty has been just *mad* for bears, ever since!). But before the show could happen, the king required my father, Master Sadiqi, to take charge of the Daluçan bear's recovery. After the long voyage

here, I'm afraid the poor dear was in the *sorriest* state..."
And the handler—a *horribly* brutal man!—had never done
the bear any good, either... but Aqib left that part out.
"Oh, from the first, Lucrio, I was so *struck* by the quick wits
of your Winterland bears. How *apt* that creature was, how
bright!"

"Aqib-sa," Lucrio cried, "*carissime puer*. Do you know
what? You just go running off at the mouth whenever
you're worried." Lucrio's eyes rendered such a fond regard, one felt abashed meeting it. "Why not tell me
what's got you so scared, then?"

Well, everything, my love. "I'm sure I don't what you
mean," Aqib said. "Now that my brother knows he must
bear our secret in silence, we've nothing to ..." Aqib assayed a shrug of nonchalance. But enough of this calling
back and forth over the fence! He stood, wiped hands
on his trousers, and left the bears' enclosure. From the
fence's gate, he gestured Lucrio to follow. "Let's see
whether we we can't find some spot where the menials
won't spy on us." His gaze flitted about as if reluctant to
meet the brown eyes of his lover. "Come on."

Lucrio came. "And that sure was something," he said,
following, "seeing your dance last night."

"No." Aqib looked back at him. "I never saw you there!
But, no, Lucrio; that just isn't possible. You can't have
been among the men, or I would have seen you."

"No, baby—upstairs," Lucrio said. "The Most High would never let us infidels onto the Sainted floor. But from upstairs in the gallery, a few of us Daluçans got to watch."

"Oh, the gallery, of course! I'd forgot all about that," Aqib said. "Do you know, I don't think I've ever been *up* there?"

"We watched from upstairs, yeah." Lucrio's fingertips traced the curve of Aqib's ear, the nape of his neck. "You were something else. Dancing like you had no bones at all, just *beautiful*. With your hips wobbling, and arms all loose, on rhythm with the drums. Some of the Olorumi ladies *cried,* watching you. And I saw one girl pass out. Even the stuck-up princess, who just came back from away, was eating you up with her eyes. But it scared me too—scared me bad, watching you. You were waaaaaay far gone." Lucrio had now taken Aqib's hand, thumb tracing his knuckles. "What was in those gourds they kept putting up to your mouth? I thought it would *kill* me when I saw you fall down like that. I thought you were dead! But our god-born knights wouldn't let me come down to you. The Corporal picked you up, and I guess he must of carried you home. At least he was gentle." Lucrio said this last with grudging fairmindedness.

All raddled and tattered like old cloth, Aqib's memory of the night before had whole events torn out of it. "I scarcely recall the benediction," he confessed. "Although I'm *very* sorry to have worried you." Behind them the big bull trumpeted, seeing Aqib so nearby: wishing him to visit. But now wasn't the time. He and Lucrio had stopped by the 'efantopia, and were somehow standing hand in hand, face to face. Here in broad daylight, where any eyes could see, Aqib had specifically meant to keep some distance between them. If anyone were to witness them thus—together—exaggerated rumor would spread with the speed of a thunderbolt. "You should not have come here, Lucrio," Aqib forced himself to say firmly. "Did you not understand the message my runner sent?"

"Yeah, I understood," Lucrio said. His fingertips seemed in thrall to the shape of Aqib's ear, tracing round and round again. "Fell asleep last night waiting for you, but this morning that runner from your place woke me up."

Aqib reached up, took grasp of the hand, and pulled it down. "Then you know that I shall come to you tonight at the fondac, as always."

"*As always*?" Lucrio looked at him strangely. "I'm gone from the fondac already, Aqib. The knights of the Tower ordered whole Embassy back to our rooms at the Sovereign House. But tonight doesn't matter; I don't care about that. What about *tomorrow* night? I keep waiting and waiting for you to say something, but the Embassy is shipping out on tomorrow's tide. Then all us Daluçans will be gone *for good,* 'member?"

Slapped to wakefulness, a sleeper jerks upright just so, slack-jawed and goggling. Aqib suffered such a rude awakening then, because he *hadn't* remembered. He'd made himself forget. These last ten days, he'd never looked further than the night ahead. Keeping to the shorter view had been trick of perspective: tonight, and tonight, and tonight being feats of wild daring, each singly, within reach of his courage. Better to forget tomorrow; better, when climbing a slope of loose gravel swarming with snakes and scorpions, to fix your eyes on the very next footfall—even if that means the cliff ahead must come as a surprise.

Seeing revelation appall Aqib's face, Lucrio pulled him in close. "Did you know: all of our unmarried knights except for one took a wife here in Olorum?" They stood close enough that these whispers seemed prelude to a kiss. "And even our great god Serra—she took the son of the Most High's brother for her man."

"Yes," Aqib said. "I'd heard."

"Well, something I bet you didn't hear: one *semidivinus* fell hard for some rich merchant's heir. After him and the boy'd been sneaking around six, seven, eight nights—just like *we* done—three months back, the boy had to run for his life to the Sovereign House, for safety-from-men. The boy's been staying there with his knight ever since. Not setting foot outside *once*—and can't, either, until we all ship out tomorrow. Or his right of sanctuary is revoked. You heard about *that*?"

"No," Aqib said.

"*We'll see our son gutted with knives, and bled out like a stuck pig making mud of dust, before we let him run off to a life without Saints.* That's what the boy's clan patricians said before the king and court."

"That should have raised the greatest scandal," Aqib said. "I wonder how no word of it has come to me?"

"Somebody didn't *want* you hearing about it," Lucrio said. "This is why Daluz wanted terms-for-love writ into the embassy treaty, or else we never would of come. The Olorumi king had to say it *plain*: any Daluçan could plight troth with any Olorumi—anybody at all—if older than first initiation and not married yet."

Aqib thought he saw where this was going. "No, Lucrio; I think not. It can well be imagined that His Holiest Majesty might allow some Daluçan to take a willing woman to wife, but men with men, *boys*—"

"*Whichever*, Aqib: we made it clear in the treaty. It's all writ down. Us Daluçans, we love too hard. We want to spend our whole life with the one we fall for. So, won't you come away with me to Terra-de-Luce tomorrow? I would stay here if I could, I swear I would. But it's another fifteen years on my tour, and Olorum's no place for two men together anyway. So please, Aqib. *Please* come with me."

It seemed the time of manageable quantities was done, and everything would now rush toward the crisis point. *No* and *yes* were equally impossible to say Instead of either, Aqib said with anguished insight, "Tell me, Lucrio: did you come here *only* to meet some Olorumi boy? *Only* to teach him your ... *modus amandi Dalucianus,* turning his face from the Saints, so that his people and family would spurn him forever?" Aqib saw that he could never be content in Olorum anymore. Where then was home? "You came here," Aqib cried out, "and *did* this to me, Lucrio?"

After a long time quiet, Lucrio said weakly, "Not *only* for that. There were a lot of reasons, Aqib ..." He mumbled a few of them: career, wealth, adventure. But obviously it was all a hedge against the true answer: *yes.* "Are you sorry then? Do you want me to go away now? Do you wish we never met at all?"

No! *Oh* no. Nonono. "No, Lucrio." Aqib spoke despairingly, holding tightly to him—to what and whom else, now? "But weren't there any boys in Daluz? Even one or two very pretty ones?"

Lucrio gave a sad crack of laughter. "Yeah, I guess some of them might of been pretty to somebody else," he said, "but for me, I needed to cross the whole *mare magnum* to find the one I was looking for."

"Racuhzin?" said some young woman, a menial appearing there beside them.

Aqib and Lucrio squeaked and leapt violently apart, in just the way no one ever does except lovers caught by surprise.

"*What?*" Aqib said, or rather shrieked.

Gaze flicking between foreign and familiar, the girl said, "You said come and get you, Racuhzin, when we was ready to clean out the ground crocs' pen. It's just that, without you keep the monsters off us, how can we get the croc shit out?"

A reasonable point. "Mm, yes," Aqib said, neatening his clothes with nervous hands. "Indeed. Well, Jellaby, you may go and tell everyone that we shall see to the ground crocs' pen *after* siesta, all right? Say to them as well that the Reverend Master's son *isn't* to be disturbed right now, for any reason. Now, away with you. Go on."

Taking her own sweet time, Jellaby backed up with luxuriously slow steps—relishing the view, the lovely scandal of it all. When she did finally face about and rush off, clearly it was neither fear nor obedience that sped her, but thrilling news.

"Aw, shit," Lucrio said. "Don't that smell like the Devil farting upwind."

"Trouble, yes," said Aqib. "Since Jellaby lies down with the Corporal whenever his wife is unwilling or with child, soon all Olorum—menial and Cousin—shall know the business of Aqib bmg Sadiqi. And know, too, with whom he transacts it." Aqib sighed tiredly and sat in the shade under the 'efantopia's fence.

Lucrio crouched on his haunches. "Daluçan law won't let us marry," he said, "of course not. But what men do—men together—is have the older one *adopt* the younger one like a son, see . . ."

"We're of the *same age,* Lucrio! You haven't reached second initiation yet either, have you?"

"No. But I *am* older: nearly twenty-two . . ."

"A couple of years! Hardly so old that you may claim to be my *father.*"

"My age ain't the *point,* Aqib! The whole adoption's just . . ." and here Lucrio groped for some word in Olorumi.

Aqib, knees drawn up and forehead resting on them, looked up. "*Pro forma,*" he said.

"Yeah! *Pro forma.* But it's just as good as marrying. Everything I have goes to you, and Daluçan law would protect you. And the whole world would know—Imperial Terra-de-Luce, anyway—what's between us. Take this back." Lucrio tossed something across to Aqib, who caught it. "Vows and papers and the rest can happen later. But if you'll have me, put that on."

It was the heavy signet ring of tarnished silver, its tourmaline seal a carved fish-shape. The thing was made for such hands as Lucrio's—mannishly thick-fingered—and would slip free at once from any of Aqib's effete digits. He turned it over in his hand. "When my father and the king were boys," Aqib said, "and all during their youth, they were the best of friends. Master Sadiqi might have married the king's sister, but he married my mother for love, instead. The Saints took my mother, who was foreign, the very same day I came to light. I know that you, Lucrio, may deem it harsh for me to say so, but for my sister and brother and me, Mother's greatest legacy has been to birth us into the fourth order of Cousins—nearly nobodies—rather than into the second, almost princes. And by custom, low-order Cousins are debarred from the court's inmost circle, from close intimacy with the king. So, Papa's ill-starred marriage also cost him—or made *very* difficult—the great friendship of his youth. My sister hasn't married yet, but no marriage of hers can lift our family up, or bring us any lower. She will take her status to her husband's family. And my brother?" Aqib joggled the ring from hand to hand, staring at it. "The Corporal met a kind-hearted girl, beautiful of face, lovely of figure. And *quite* young, my brother married her. He does love his wife very much; but she too is only a Cousin of the fourth order."

"So they want *you* to marry some high girl, then?" Lucrio said. "A princess?"

"Yes. If I marry well and before my sister does, all *her* prospects are made the brighter. And the Corporal . . ." Aqib made a face: showing what, exactly? Love of family, ancient pain, hero-worship, and terrible pain all over again—this succession flitted through Aqib's heart and across his face. "I regret, Lucrio, that you've never seen the Corporal at his best. But sometimes he has been wonderfully kind to me. He's been the best brother anyone could have wished for. Sad to say—and a great difference, I know, from your Daluçan meritocracy—advancement in the armies of Olorum owes mostly to one's status among the cousinry, and very little to a warrior's native capacities. Truly, the Corporal is a lion at war, a master of every martial art: he *deserves* to make a great career in the armies. But he never will—indeed *can*not—unless I thicken the family's blood with a good marriage."

While listening, Lucrio shook his head slowly, then with increasing vehemence. "That's what the Corporal must of *told* you, Aqib. But listen. I spent this whole last season with the Olorumi armies, and I met *plenty* of captains, high captains, and even one marshal who came up out of the undercity: no sort of Cousin at all. And your brother? He ain't no lion at war—a *nasty bully* is what he is! Just because he's always ready to hurt somebody weaker, don't believe he knows *one damn thing* about war-arts. You saw us fight at the fondac, didn't you? Me tossing him around like nothing? You *saw* that. The *stupid* way he charged in with that spear! Do you know I never once saw your brother with the Olorumi soldiers—the *serious ones*—when I was teaching our Daluçan *manu aperta*? And the pathetic way he fights hand-to-hand, the Corporal don't know shit about your Kapoway style, either!" Almost spitting with scorn, Lucrio said: "Calling hisself 'the Corporal.' By now, his sorry ass should be *Captain,* if he was any good!" Lucrio did spit then, off to the side. "Which he ain't."

This tirade hit Aqib not unlike a blow to the belly. It hurt cruelly to hear one he loved speak so ill of another equally loved. Aqib grabbed fistfuls of his pants' loose material to still his trembling hands. "The Corporal may not be the most excellent of men," he said, "or even of soldiers. I only know that I love my brother. That's all I know, Lucrio. Master Sadiqi my father, however, truly *is* the best and kindest man in Olorum. That I be born alive, his beloved wife had to die. Yet my father has only ever shown me gentle forbearance. Can't you see, Lucrio? I'm only a small-game hunter, and no sort of warrior at all.

But still I shall become Master of Beasts and the Hunt after my father. Why? Because Master Sadiqi chose to pass all the secrets of his mastery on to me. He is *everything* good, in one person." Resolve entered Aqib's voice as he spoke. He extended a hand to Lucrio, the ring held out. "I cannot sail away with you and the Daluçans." As one does to shore up weak conviction, Aqib shook his head as spoke. "To abandon my family, my father: it would be the worst sort of betrayal. I cannot do it, Lucrio. I'm sorry."

Lucrio reached and closed Aqib's hand around the ring. "Your papa," Lucrio said in a crude tone, making an ugly face, "—is he wicked or just a *fool,* Aqib?"

Lucrio had never before spoken words so like a personal attack, but Aqib found he could extend the benefit of the doubt even here. As if preparing to laugh at some joke, he smiled uncertainly. "You are jesting," Aqib said. "What can you mean, my love?"

"I mean, you keep saying how wonderful your papa is. But can you tell me why, all the years of your life, the Corporal's just been whaling on you, but your papa never knew, and never stopped it? Or does Master Sadiqi know just fine, Aqib? Does he want you thinking, 'Oh, Papa's the gentle one. Papa's the one who's nice to me.' But also he likes the Corporal doing all the dirty work, every mean thing. The breaking, the beating, the cruelness. That's what I think. That Master Sadiqi's as bad and worse than the Corporal, Aqib. Full of games and tricks!"

"I thought I had a friend in you." Aqib stood abruptly, his voice raised. "How can you speak this way to me?" Aqib flung the ring. "You should leave here, Lucrio. Go now!" *Not for one moment had Papa been a refuge, but all along the overseer and source of pain.*

Nasty and high-handed as he'd been a moment ago, Lucrio now became just that humble. Sometimes lovers err and learn the limits too late, however. Aqib strode swiftly from the heart of the Menagerie, toward a spot on its western wall: site of the secret door. Recanting his slander, pleading and making promises, Lucrio followed. O youthful urgencies! O passions of first love! How the years have wearied one's heart and dimmed the memories. How, this old man wonders, can that boy have been so angry, when his lover only spoke the truth?

"When the ship gets back to Daluz," Lucrio said, "the Senate will give me a lifetime boon. I'll never be a poor man again, Aqib. We couldn't live the way you're used to here, but I swear, you'd never go hungry with me, never go without." This was one of a thousand desperate assurances Lucrio made to him during that last walk together. "There'd be some luxury, too, from time to time. And later on, I promise, we'd have much better money. I'm young and my star's going up. Someday as high as Consul, maybe. Everything mine would be yours: Daluçan law says so. You'd never be penniless, no matter what."

Money? As other peoples did not fret whether air-to-breathe would suffice tomorrow, a royal cousin never worried about money. There was more wealth in the Kingdom of Olorum than in the world's remainder combined. Aqib might have explained that every Cousin was a trustee of the Royal Treasury, beneficiary of millions or billions according to status, and by birthright, at any time, could cash out his or her full share. That, of course, meant slamming shut the open doors to power, and trading one's status as a royal cousin for hard currency. But still, if he and Lucrio ran away together, they certainly needn't do so as paupers.

Aqib observed himself failing to mention this—failing to say anything at all—as Lucrio belabored what he must imagine were the practical concerns. "Hush, Lucrio," Aqib said, when they arrived at the Menagerie's walls. Two gargantuan trees there had grown together—or one massive tree, twin-trunked. "Right now I can't hear you. My anger is too great." He felt sick with confusion. Aqib wanted the solace only Lucrio could give; an embrace, a kiss, whispers that all would be well. But he also just wanted to see the back of him. "I shall come to you tonight at the Sovereign House. Then, we may make our proper good-byes." Aqib marveled that he could feel so wholly persuaded by the sight of his beloved weeping in remorse; and yet still, in manner and speech, seem piti-less. "For now, I need you gone."

Lucrio said he thought their last chance was right this moment, that if Aqib might change his mind, after all, and wish to go with the Daluçan ship, then even a little while later could prove too late. Tonight might never come for them. At the time, Aqib heard no word of this. Only thinking back in after years did regret remind him what Lucrio had said. Then, he put hands on Lucrio and pushed him—Lucrio letting himself be pushed—toward the deep seam between the great fused tree boles. Lucrio pressed the ring back into Aqib's hand.

"Bring it to me tonight, if you won't keep it."

Aqib nodded.

Lucrio hummed the proper note. As some discreet nib-bler takes in a morsel of food with lips barely ajar, just so, one tree trunk pursed slightly away from the other, and that seam of rough bark writhed with a masticatory action: the strange mouth beginning to engorge Lucrio, hands, arms, head, trunk... Perplexing the mind, this paradox baffled the eyes, for the aperture never seemingly widened far enough to admit a burly, broad-shouldered man. Yet Lucrio passed easily between the tree trunks, disappearing within—and through—to emerge outside the Menagerie. From the wall's far side there came a faint call, *Ego te amo*. Aqib turned back to the chores of his stewardship.

[*52 YEARS OLD*]

"Does my papa ail, Blessèd Mother? Why does he sit that way, so still and staring ahead? He won't answer me, Mama. He doesn't move!"

"Do not be alarmed, Lucretia. Your father was becoming very unhappy, and we've only made it so he can be glad again. By the orderly strength of your mind, I see that the women of the Sovereign House have already taught you something of telepathy, haven't they? So you will understand when I say, all we have done is take one nasty little memory from your papa's head, so that it should no longer bother him, and make him sad."

"I do not *like* this, Mama, I don't!"

"Lucretia, be still. You shall comport yourself acceptably. Are you crying? I won't *have* it!"

"No, Mama—I will do. I'm not."

"Then fix your face, girl, and sit up."

"O Blessèd among Olorumi, she cannot help herself; the child is becoming overwrought. Shall we tranq her, too? We cannot extirpate a mind so well trained as hers, but we can certainly calm the child. One so young shouldn't likely remember the experience. Shall we do it?"

Lucretia wept wretchedly.

"Yes; if it will stop that sniveling. And *free* him. It's too eerie how he sits there thus, so still. No, wait!—now, his heart lies bare for you to read, I would wish to know a thing."

"Ah, no, Blessèd Femysade. We cannot. We may not answer such questions. A telepath of the Ashëan Enclave must uphold its ethos, for each offense perturbs her mind's clarity, until she's rendered incapable of fine work and subtleties. Therefore I can reveal none of your husband's secrets to you."

"Of course. I understand. The elastic of your ethics stretches far enough to promote your own interests in these negotiations, but, unfortunately, snaps back just short of answering a question of mine. Have I got that right? Stow the bullshit, maga. And you will answer my question in the Inflection of Truth. I wish to know whether my husband loves me."

"We should not answer, O Blest."

"You *shall*, though, if you cherish any hope of persuading me across the bayou."

"Then I would answer you that he does, O Blest. Indeed, just now he meant to beseech you to stay in Olorum—for the child's sake, yes, but also for his own. For love of you."

"But do I stand . . . first in his regard? I love no other; does he?"

"Sanctified Cousin Aqib bmg Sadiqi sees himself, first of all, a father—and so the Blessèd Lucretia stands foremost in his heart. Now, I beg you: no more questions. Strenuous expiations will be required for me to recover pellucidity. I have already trespassed further than I ever have before."

"And yet, not nearly far enough. You call me *savant,* but seek to play me for a fool. You haven't *answered* the question, maga. That a father may care for his daughter, my own child, is well and fine; who objects? But I am speaking—as you are perfectly aware—of the love between man and woman. *Passion.* Now, answer me again, and answer straight. No sophistry, no split hairs."

"Then no, Femysade. Your answer is *no.* You were not his first, nor are you best with him. Before you were married there was another, and your husband . . . does not forget."

"I knew there was some woman before me; I *felt* it. At one moment he seemed to know nothing of love, but the next, far too much. I *knew!*"

The gods said nothing.

"And has he . . . has my husband ever played me false?"

"We will answer you in this, O Blest, but thereafterwards you must stay in Olorum, as you so choose—never knowing such wonders as the children of Ashê would have plied you with—for I will *not* pry further into your husband's mind. Aqib bmg Sadiqi has been faithful to you, from the day your broker put forward the proposal, unto this one: never touching another, never secretly intriguing to do so."

"But he did love a woman before me, and loves her better even now. You said so." The Blessèd Femysade muttered to herself. "Why should I stay then, what holds me here? You *said* so ... Wake him."

. . . storm-tossed, his ship wrecking in the doldrums of forgetfulness, after many voyages in dreamlands, Aqib fetched up finally ashore, at home—sweaty, foul-mouthed after siesta, tangled in the sheets of his own bed. He sat up and clapped twice. Menials brought rinse water to him, and a chewing-stick to freshen teeth and breath. They laid out the afternoon robe of an Olorumi grandee, the black matte linen, its embroidery gleaming. Aqib washed, dressed, and he'd ... dreamt perhaps? No, *certainly*. He was sure he'd dreamt of the Daluçan Garden again; for that metallic savor lingered in his mouth, and in his spirit an inexplicable melancholy, a hauntedness. Not the first such dream—perhaps the *thousandth*; but as always, he could recall little detail from the dream. So often recurring, never remembered? What did the dream concern, precisely? Voices, the gods, his daughter weeping ... Aqib's utter conviction, on the one hand, and complete confusion, on the other, kindled a queasy stir in his belly, a pounding in his head. Only three mortals could speak to the events in the Daluçan Garden that day: one of them dead, and another himself, full of doubts. Aqib went down to the nursery to put his questions to the Blessèd Lucretia.

He'd proved to be a difficult witch, this newborn prince. No indeed: he'd take no teat in the world except his own mother's, and he had terrorized all his early nurses, daily blasting the nursery to Kingdom come. Prostrate and tearful, Lucretia appealed at last to her dearest friend, who came to the rescue. Now "Nurse," the former chief translator at the Sovereign House had abandoned the pompous honors of her old office. She was no longer a voice of elegant fluency heard in every foreign negotiation, but only bodywoman to a frazzled, first-time mother; no master, anymore, of linguists, scholars, and wisewomen, but only mistress of a tikky infant's ransacked nursery.

She was alone with the child when Aqib entered. Without Lucretia there, the usual chaos reigned in the baby's room. Everything upended itself, strew itself, flapping or tumbling under its own will. Nurse was the image, still, of immaculate pulchritude, even in this humble post. She stood in the middle of pandemonium, hands clutched in her lovely skirts.

"But where is my grandson?" Aqib asked her.

Lucretia's woman pointed, Aqib's gaze following her finger.

Sweet Saints. Oh, dear! This was a thing Lucretia certainly had never done.

Olorum's prince rolled himself over belly to back, and over again, gurgling happily, as any child his age might do on the floor. Except the Blessèd prince played on the ceiling.

"Sometimes the child will lose control unexpectedly," Aqib cautioned. "One shudders to imagine him falling from such a height. Perhaps it were better, then, if you brought him down from there."

Nurse looked from the child, to Aqib beside her. Such work must, of course, be frustrating for one who had once known far more august labors. One could observe the harried woman's struggle for composure and words. "Yes, *thank you,* Sanctified Cousin. I do think you have the right of it; I'd *quite* thought so too! How then would the Reverend Master suggest I go about bringing the Blessèd prince down?"

Erm, ah . . . The ceiling loomed about four tall-men's-height above them.

Aqib confessed himself at a loss.

"Perhaps," said Nurse, "*you,* Cousin, might ask the prince (may all Saints bless him) to come down to us? He listens to you more than anyone."

Not so much anymore; but Aqib stretched his hands up toward his grandson. *Will you not come down—softly, gently—to visit with me, dear child?* There was a little interval after birth, Aqib had found, when mortal children were entirely animal, and could be spoken to and persuaded just as Aqib might any animal. That interval was brief, however, and soon infants crossed over into a wholly other state, where he could not reach them except by way of ordinary babble. The prince said, "Baba!" and grinned, his little fat fist waving. "Baba!" *Papa* was what he called the King of Olorum, City and Nation. Happily the prince would offer his greetings, but still he declined to come down.

"I think," Aqib said, "that we'd better call in his mother, the Blessèd Lucretia."

"Oh, but she was awake most of the night," Nurse said, "and only *just* lay down for siesta! I'd hoped to let her rest awhile."

There was no help for it, though. Aqib stepped into the hallway and sent a menial scurrying to fetch his daughter. He and Nurse brushed aside dancing sheets and clothing, skirted tumbling furniture, trying to keep directly under the child as he rolled about the ceiling.

She had, of course, been through the wars; but never had she so much looked it. Haggard and bleary-eyed, Lucretia appeared in the nursery doorway. Milk stained her shirt, her trousers worn down to threadbare softness (for she'd kept these—preferring them—since girlhood).

"*Qary-sa!*" Lucretia cried, looking upwards. "Come down from there. Come *down,* I say." The chaos in the room stilled at a waved hand, which she then stretched toward the ceiling. Her son ceased to roll about, but he didn't descend. Lucretia frowned. Hand still raised, she came into the room.

"What is it?" Nurse said. "You cannot bring him down?"

"Oh, *excellent,*" Lucretia said with bitter incredulity. "This was the only thing lacking! Now, Qary resists when I try to counter his antics."

Aqib didn't like the worried note in his daughter's voice. "But surely the child isn't stronger than you?" he said, inwardly thanking the Saints, again, that witchcraft had come upon his daughter so much later, as a sensible child of eight years.

"No, not that," said Lucretia. "Or *not yet,* I should say. Saints forbid! But . . . imagine snatching something from a child. Only you must imagine that 'something' delicately lodged within the child's body." Very slowly, and laughing the while, sometimes bobbing upwards a little ways again, the prince came floating down. "Ever so gently . . . lest I do him an injury," Lucretia said. Until lately she'd been used to employing her witchcraft only to mighty effect: war and hunting, exerting brute force on great weights. Finesse was plainly taxing to her. Tremors faintly shook her out-stretched hand, and biting her lower lip, she spoke no more during the Blessèd prince's descent. At length, son settled into mother's arms, and decided at once that he was famished, and must nurse *now*. Lucretia held the fussing baby propped on one arm: "Just a moment, dear love," she said, other hand fumbling at her shirt laces. "Mama will see you fed in just a ..." The air seethed with uncanny spirits, and Aqib fell back in alarm, Nurse giving a little shriek. Invisible power—laces popping suddenly, unraveling, snapping like snakes—wrenched apart the halves of Lucretia's shirt. "The Saints slept!" she cursed, not in anger but exhaustion.

"Lucretia mln Femysade!" Aqib said, appalled by this vile hersey. (For, by Canon, the Saints never sleep but are ever-vigiliant: watching the whole of creation at *all* times ...) "Such *language*! I will thank you to remember that you're not amongst soldiers on a battlefield!"

"Oh, pardon me, Papa," cried his daughter, the baby already at her breast and snuffling contentedly. "I do forget myself sometimes, Master Aqib." Lucretia touched a fingertip to her son's busy cheek, and stroked tenderly, shedding a tear or two of *mater in extremis*. "I fear I'm at my wit's end ..." And the Right-Hand Witch *was* sadly come down from her days of battlefield glory, when once she'd single-handedly covered an army's retreat, saving the life of the Most Holy in the days when he'd still only been prince.

"Sit yourself then, O Blessèd among Olorumi," said Lucretia's woman, embracing her—guiding them both down onto pillows. "Sit and rest awhile." Lucretia leaned against the smaller woman; and held by her, shed a few more tears. Aqib felt moved, at last, to endorse the notion he'd so often railed against.

"We shall do as Nurse has suggested," Aqib said briskly. "Let us send to the Ashëan Enclave. The gods will surely know better than we how to care for a baby with tikky."

"TK, Papa," Lucretia said, "telekinesis."

"Mmhm," Aqib said. "Just so. Daughter, if you tell the Most Holy that his Blessèd son requires such aid as only the gods can give, then the king will straightaway send a herald speeding across the bayou." Her Grace, the wife of His Holiest Majesty, had birthed one daughter after another, five in all now. Lucretia's child was the only son.

"I will do so tonight, Master Aqib," Lucretia said. "His Holiest Majesty means to stop in after prayers. I'll tell him then." She gave Aqib a look of teary gratitude. "Thank you, Papa, *thank you.*"

"Hush, child," Aqib said gently. "Soon everything will be well." He felt no love for the gods, but as unstintingly as a father and grandfather could feel, Aqib loved his daughter and grandson. For Lucretia and Qary, he could swallow his hate. Olorum had never known such virulently powerful witches before that fateful day in the Daluçan Garden, when his family met with the prophet and the maga. As one who hadn't forgiven, not yet or ever, Aqib said, "The gods still owe us a favor or two, I daresay."

Nurse said, "Oh, do you feel they've shorted us, then, Sanctified Cousin? Really, I'd thought the Ashëans have dealt with Olorum most *open-handedly*," she exclaimed. "The lovely extended canals! This new pavement, smooth and uncracking, over all the streets and boulevards: what a wonder it is! And have you gone yet to tour the seaside citadel, now the construction's finally done? Oh, see it, Reverend Master, *do*! I swear it is an *aweful* prodigy—!" Quellingly Lucretia grasped her woman's hand, just as Aqib snapped,

"They took more than they gave!"

This sort of outburst will beget awkward silence, but grandfather, mother, and Nurse had plenty to fill up the lull, putting the nursery back into order. The prince spit some milk onto Lucretia's shoulder and fell asleep; she passed him to his nurse, who laid him down in the depression—softly pillowed—delved out of a massive granite block. Here was a cradle the little witch couldn't hurl about the room while dreaming. Lucretia picked through heaped and scattered clothing for another shirt. Sooner would the menials flee the house howling than enter into the haunted nursery. Therefore it fell to them to right overturned bureau, table, stools . . . When they'd all sat down together, folding mother and baby clothes, Aqib told them of his worrisome dream.

". . . but I woke this afternoon convinced the dream *has* come to me before, and come again and again. Ever since that day in the Daluçan Garden. Mad as it may sound, I would almost say that it feels as if there were a . . . *whole episode* missing from my memory of that day. As if asleep I can remember it, but once awake, the event slides away, rather like"—here his hands motioned, illuminating his words—"a fish might elude an ill-cast net." Aqib bent his aching head (oh, it *pained* him!) and pressed a hand lightly to the roiling nausea in his belly.

"O Sanctified Cousin, I would ask," said Nurse, very quietly: "Do you suffer feelings of vertigo and sun-dazzlement when you seek to remember that day?"

Aqib, who held temples pinched between thumb and forefinger, eyes squinted against a sudden glare, looked up sharply. "Yes! How did you know, Nurse? Tell me."

Lucretia and her woman looked speakingly to each other. His daughter spoke. "Papa—truly I was so young then. I confess that what I remember best is having so badly to *pee,* and very little of what occurred, what was said. Two beautiful giants . . . ? You calling a pretty yellow bird to your finger . . . ? But the gods *do* take advantage of men sometimes . . ."

"Darling." Lucretia's woman set a hand upon her arm. "You know very well that you cannot—"

"We are speaking, Enghélasade, of my *father*!" Lucretia pulled her arm free, and said to Aqib in a great rush, "Because you are so strong a psion, I suspect a geas the gods laid took poorly. They did a thing to you they can only do to men—to the untrained, Papa. In the Sovereign House we learn too many counters, I mean we women and girls, against mnemonic extirpation and coercive psionics generally, and so no geas can . . ."

"Slowly, Daughter." Aqib's head swam from sickness and the flood of women's argot. "I cannot follow you. 'Mnemonic extirpation'—what is that, exactly? And, tell me; what are these 'coercive psionics'? Explain to me this thing 'geas,' if you please."

Nurse murmured again, "*Lucretia*": the softest and yet monitory exhortation.

"They are . . . ," and his daughter gave a defeated sigh. Her fatigue suddenly seemed to double as she slumped with exhaustion. " . . . They are the stuff and business of women, Master Aqib." She seized Aqib's hand and pulled him nearer to her—to kiss his forehead, kiss both his cheeks. "I really may not say, Papa. Oh, it's a *mad, ugly* world we live in, isn't it? Men and women, side by side, yet further apart than this earth from the stars ... ! But as you love me, Papa—as you value your own sanity—let the dreams come as they will, and never seek to ponder on them. Don't pick at the edges of your memory. *Please* don't, Papa. I'm sure you feel strongly impelled to let it all simply pass away—to forget—don't you? Well, *do that.* Just let it all go, Papa."

The fog of forgetfulness would indeed be easy to sink into, but Aqib wished fiercely to know *more,* to understand *better.* Then he saw an expression on his daughter's face he recognized well, for he'd worn it from time to time himself. It was the careworn look of love wise parents wear, when they know better, when they know this most willful child of theirs is racing toward catastrophe. Lucretia was a woman, but she was wise; no one could deny that. The king himself came round night and day, *What about this, O Blest, what about that? Should I, Lucretia, should I not?* So Aqib nodded.

He left the women with the prince in the nursery and went out to his garden, where the menials spread a picnic for him. Among the flowers, in the shade, he sang down a parakeet. Bribing her with a morsel, he asked the bird go and inform his niece and nephew, in plainly spoken Olorumi, that Uncle would be around to the Menagerie before dusk to check upon their work.

The dreams might have come again after that day, but Aqib never remembered. He let the matter go.

[*TENTH NIGHT*]

In his bedchamber Aqib lay atop the sheets, joggling his mother's emeralds in one hand. He *must* go now. If he would make this valediction at all, it were best done while the household settled in after midnight prayers. Under cover of darkness, he could leave, return, and never be missed. "Goodbye, Lucrio," he'd say, "I cannot do it." He would *mean* what he said: "I am bound by duty to my family, and I cannot abandon them." Very likely Lucrio would embrace him then, kiss his mouth, and say, "*Please.*" And how brown his eyes would be, how soft his beard . . . Aqib trembled.

He would always doubt, after tonight, quite what he'd meant to do. He fully intended *not* to sail away with the Daluçans. And so his answer to Lucrio would have been, "No." And yet, "Yes"; for what chance that a whisper and kiss wouldn't have persuaded him otherwise? Could the weak glue of a "No" have held under the pressure of a softly spoken "*Please*"?

Oh, doubtful, Aqib.

Doubtful.

As he was *not* going, Aqib didn't permit himself to pack clothing or pilfer into a pocket any little keepsake from among his effects. He meant to give back the ring, loose about his right thumb, and then come straightaway back to his father's house.

Skin flush with bliss, chilling in dread, Aqib sat up in the bed. Pressing a hand to his cramping guts, he rose.

A sentimental boy about to fly abroad with his lover would never leave behind these emeralds. He simply couldn't, a boy of such sentiment. Therefore Aqib made himself stow the jewels back into their box, the box back into its place. Love of the Saints, *why* hadn't they extinguished the lamps by the gate yet? Always before, the houseguard had put them out by this hour. Aqib flung off his sumptuous prayer robes and threw on workaday shirt and trousers. Lest his chamber attendant wake, he crept quietly through his apartments, quietly through the house, and out into the front courtyard. When Aqib neared the gate, a shadow detached itself from the abundant dark, and stepped into the lamp-light—stepped into the way: the Reverend Master Sadiqi. "And where are you rushing off to, my son?" said his father. "At this most unhallowed hour of the night?"

Taken by surprise, Aqib loosed a little scream. A sinner

might so tremble before the apparition of his Saint. "Oh, Master Sadiqi!" Aqib said, trying for a bright, pleasant tone. "How you startled me! I was just going . . ." Yes, where, Aqib? To go and make wanton, desperate love to your Daluçan for the last time? To cover his lips and cheeks and forehead with kisses and tears? To caress his body from head to toe? To give back the ring you really ought to keep, as his boy, as his lifetime lover: for, here, in this time and place, belated relevation has come to you at last? As long as you live, no better chance for wholly congenial partnership will ever come to you. So flee with your Lucrio—*flee*! Is that where you're going, Aqib? "I wanted to . . . I had only thought . . ." His father stood in patient expectancy, as if to see what latest canard should emerge from his son. When Aqib could hit upon no ready alibi, he fell quiet. A good boy can jive and justify only so long before he finds his mouth capable of truth or silence, but no more lies.

"These rumors that come to my ears," said Master Sadiqi, "are *shocking*, Aqib. And though one *strives* to give the gossips no credit, I must say it would greatly aid my efforts—and give vicious tongues *ever* so much less to talk about—if you retired to your rooms straight after prayers, and *slept* there"—the master's voice shading with a suggestion of the vile things boys got up to when they slept where they oughtn't—"in your own bed till morning. So, let's be having you back off to your rooms, then, yes? I'll just stand here and watch you walk inside, I think. And we'd better set a guard, have the men lock the compound's gate, and paint it with the Saint-sign, too. For my heart is weighing heavy, Aqib. I fear the Devil walks abroad tonight. I fear lest He enter *here*, into our own abode, and perhaps carry off some son of ours. So go back to your rooms now, boy. Go!"

But Aqib didn't go. He stood there, mind wracking itself for any pretext—other than blazing hot sin—on which a wild-eyed seventeen-year-old, all sweaty and in a fret, might rush out of his father's home in the wee hours of the morning.

Haughty and grand, a king's-friend and former Cousin of the second order, Master Sadiqi transformed before Aqib's eyes. From one moment to the next, his father became a quite elderly man, white-headed and weary, a widower whose beloved wife had died birthing this, his favorite child. Which boy was running wild these last few nights, and bringing down all manner of shame upon the house. "Will you not go to your rooms, my son?" said Master Sadiqi sadly.

Aqib felt in his heart that his father, this man, had done right by him all the days of his life, and been kind, too—no matter what Lucrio had said.

"*Please*, Aqib," said his father.

Been good and kindly . . . and yet Aqib wanted Lucrio. Did he want him enough to shove past his own father, throwing the old man aside in order to flee . . . ?

Yes!

He made to lunge but then saw the shadows shift. In the greater dark whereoutfrom his father had stepped, Aqib realized the Corporal and two burliest of the house-guard were standing at the ready, tensed to come to the aid of the Reverend Master. There had never been a possibility that Aqib would leave this compound tonight. *This is our chance,* Lucrio had pled at the Menagerie. *Come with me now, if you'll come at all.* Aqib couldn't remember a single one of his stupid reasons for not going with Lucrio then. He turned without a word and went back to his rooms.

Kneeling beside the bed, he rolled his mother's emeralds in his hand. Three cabochons, each as big as a thumb pad; Mother had doubtlessly meant them for some finished piece of jewelry. Yet we can but propose, it being for the Saints to dispose. As an infant, Aqib had once been allowed to play with the jewels, and then cried and clung so fiercely that Mother's emeralds had somehow remained in his holding all these years, though Sister was dowered with all the rest of Mother's effects. Their monetary value meant nothing to Aqib; their worth lay in power to comfort. To roll the emeralds in his hand as a baby and child, and now as a man, had many times eased insupportable anguish to a hurt he could bear. How would his mother have spoken on all this? For all Aqib knew, it could be that Always-Walking-People, like the Daluçans, had very different taboos. Unconditional acceptance might be had from a mother you'd never known and could only imagine: that was these emeralds' power. But even these Aqib would throw away, if it meant he might sail off with Lucrio—or even just say goodbye properly, without anger. Aqib knew the history of Lucrio's signet ring, a last heirloom of his forefathers, and therefore precious beyond price. How faithless would he think Aqib! Never showing up, and yet *keeping* the ring . . . Only to return it, he'd willingly give up Mother's emeralds.

Would he?

According to household rumor, the newest of his father's guardsmen was a raw peasant from the countryside, and miserable here in the City. The man longed to go back home, but owed Master Sadiqi fourteen and a half years on a fifteen-year bond. The plan Aqib hatched was hopeless if that guardsman was on duty tonight. But if *free* . . . Aqib rose and woke his chamber attendant, sending the menial to fetch the guardsman to him. "And do it quietly, with *discretion*."

His attendant showed the man into Aqib's antechamber. The guardsman arrived rumpled from sleep; and how rough-skinned he was, how painfully thin! The man exhibited that ineffable deficit of health and beauty prevailing in the lowest caste. With a fingersnap, Aqib dismissed the prying eyes and pricked-up ears of his attendant back to a sleeping alcove in a further room. Late-night summons into private quarters perforce evoke a sense of the greatest intimacy. Therewith ill-at-ease, and with the luxe of the surroundings, the nervous guardsman grinned hideously, crouching on his haunches.

"I would ask a great favor," said Aqib, low-voiced (for it seemed the whole world was always listening in). "And in turn I would do a great favor for you. Whether you say *No* or *Yes* to me, either way, no harm shall come to you. Will you hear me, guardsman?"

"Begging your pardon, Racuhzin . . ." The man licked chapped lips, glancing fearfully right and left. "But the Reverend Master Sadiqi, and Racuhzin the Corporal—"

"—must never know we have spoken," Aqib interrupted. He rolled emeralds round and round in his own nervous hand. "I have heard that you wish to return to your home. That you'd like to see your family again, the friends you love, and the places you know. Well, I am the only one who can help you. There *are* no others. The rest who can do not care. So, will you hear me, guardsman?"

A frightened grimace, those *wretched* teeth . . . ! At last, the guardsman nodded.

"I require you to go, tonight, to the Sovereign House. Go to the wing where the Embassy is quartered: go to the western gate. Fear not to meet the king's men; there will be only Daluçans manning that gate. Say to them that you bear a message for the tricenturion Lucrio Cordius de Besberibus, and the Daluçans will bring that man before you." *Passing fine he will be, too. With brown hair shimmering in the lantern-light.* "Say to him that I, Aqib bmg Sadiqi, bid him farewell and safe voyage. Say that I grieve to be unable to come in my own person. Give to him this ring I wear on my hand. And then say . . ." *I love you I love you I love you I'm sorry.* But no, Aqib: this messenger can say no more than you have already given him. "If you will do this thing for me, I swear I'll see you come into monies to repay your bond to my father in full. By the blood of All Saints, I swear that even before the Long Rains fall you shall win free of this household, this City, and be on your way home again."

But the guardsman only crouched and gaped. Thought moving behind men's eyes ordinarily betrays itself in some glimmer: *here,* no such light. A vacancy looked back at Aqib—deaf and dumb. Could the proposed subterfuge have so terrified the guardsman, he could not even *refuse* the errand? Nor would such terror be entirely ill-founded, for Aqib was the very least of powers in this household. The Master's hand might lie gently, for the most part; but the Corporal's . . .

Oh, Aqib would have liked to jump up and smash the appointments of his rooms, while railing at life's injustice. He would have like to be stretched out beside Lucrio, exhausted after love-making, knowing that in the morning the Daluçan ship would bear them both away to whatever new places, new adventures. He would have liked anything better than to be begging this, *this* . . . Just when Aqib would have given up the gambit and dismissed the houseguard from his chambers, there came a little nod, and the whispered words: "I'll do it, Racuhzin."

[**89 YEARS OLD**]

Nights had little sleep in them. Aqib would lie down waiting for his eyes to shut, but sleep always came later and more briefly. Regrets would poke him in the darkness, until he got up to wander about his palace and its grounds by touch and squinted gaze. Lately he was going further afield, down into the undercity, the hour of night notwithstanding.

Boss? Old Benj sat up. *Where are you going?*

Aqib fought, failed and at last managed to rise. *For a walk.*

Let me go and wake the bitch or her puppy or one of his. Will you not go with someone?

Alone, Aqib said shortly, *or with you.*

But it's darkest night, and the nose says storms, maybe.

I would walk; I cannot sleep!

This gallivanting. You're a weak old hound now, boss, gray and shaky.

Struggling on his robe, Aqib snapped, *So are you.*

Then have we not earned some rest in these last waning nights?

Stay here, if you've grown too old. I shall go on alone.

Old Benj sighed, and tottered afoot himself. *I will always go with you. Whither lions and snakes, into black insipid silence, unto mine ending or past yours.*

You old poet. Aqib put down his hand. *Best of friends. The very best you are.* He would rather have stooped down, to take this kiss on his cheeks and chin not fingers, but Aqib felt sure that all his up-and-downing was finished now. Just once more, and only down.

His household slept, menials and Cousins alike. The guard were at the front gate, not the postern door. For the last time he and Old Benj walked slowly and alone into night.

He awoke in blue gloom, slow to remember (which) self, where (in space), when (in youth, in age) he was. Himself; the Sybil's cave, poorly lit by weak godslight; soon to celebrate forty years of life. He was in Daluz. *This* was his life, wherein he'd only known contentment—up until the fierce onset, in the last year or two, of second thoughts.

But where were they now? The anguish and desperation he'd felt earlier this same morning, when he'd begged the Sybil: "Did I choose right? Or should I have stayed in Olorum?" No regrets, now! He wanted no life but the one he'd lived!

"Well?" The Sybil stirred in her glass. "There it is," she said. "Such life as you'd have lived, if you'd chosen Olorum." There was no saying how one knew her for female, for the Sybil's speech was inaudible, of projected image and emotion, of alien thoughts sent into the mind. And dark was the glass of her jar, dim the shape within it; scaled, grotesque, nothing human. "Now you've lived to the end of that other path, do you still covet it?"

Aqib made to speak and found, as when one has breathed by mouth the night through, his tongue all pasty, and throat utterly dry. He had to work his tongue awhile to rouse enough spit to answer. "No," Aqib said.

Then he reached out a hand suddenly, grasping at nothing. "My daughter!"

The Sybil mocked this outcry. "Not yours," she said. "The pride and joy of that other man. *You* are daughterless."

That was just noise to Aqib. His heart spat it out for nonsense. Lucretia had clutched no fingers but *his*, toddling her first few steps. *He* had carried her bloody to the healers, when she'd faced down and slain the marauding lion. And *he'd* spoken such bitter words—though in truth admiring her, envying her—when she'd refused marriage to her cousin, the Most Holy of Olorum, City and Nation, in favor of unwedded freedom. They were his grandson, *his* great-grandchildren ... but in *this* life there were two other, more proximate youngsters, weren't there? Covering his face with his hands, Aqib said, "It was just a dream, only a dream ..."

Croakingly the Sybil laughed. "No indeed!" she said. "It's you who are the dream, that other man who is flesh and real, the dreamer."

Existential horror seized Aqib. At her words, he thought he might vomit forth his soul onto the floor, and his body break up into its constituencies: here a soft heap of empty flesh, there neatly stacked bones, his glistening organs all colorfully in a row, and the divided whole of him pooled around by lacquered blood ... That *other*

Aqib was the dream, or *he* was?

Giddy with malice, the Sybil clicked her talons against the jar's insides, then scratched dreadfully at the glass. "*You're* the dream," she cackled. "*He* is real!"

And didn't Aqib remember longing for this self and this life and these outcomes, mere fantasies? Then how, but who . . . ? His sanity rattled like a shack in high winds, verging on collapse. What shored him up was the memory of Lucrio's warning. "The Sybil never lies. But she tricks you with sly and partial truth, leaving out the crucial piece. *Sic cave, mi carissime; cave!* The Sybil drives many petitioners mad . . ." Aqib's saving thought: *I am the dream but so is he.* And that felt right to him, as did the thought: *He is real but so am I.*

The madness abated, and with it the Sybil's gleeful tantrum. "So then," she said resentfully, "did I requite your question, Aqib amans Lucrionis? Did I answer to your satisfaction?"

Face cupped in the bowl of his hands, he said, "Yes."

"Then I find my mind changed," said the Sybil. "Now, I want the whole of your hand."

Aqib's head snapped up. "You said one finger only!"

"Very well." The Sybil spoke as if indifferent. "You may keep your hand and fingers all. I'll just have back what you know of that other life, and the value of its lessons, too. Does that suit you?"

It didn't, no. Untopping his little pot of honey, sticking a finger in—a hollow knock inside the glass; a jolt that rocked the jar; the Sybil shrieked, "The *whole* of your hand!"—Aqib scooped out a fat and glistening dollop onto his other hand, stickily smearing palm, the back, and every finger. He climbed onto the high stool. He leaned against the rough thick glass and reached his left arm up to the mouth of the great jar, then bent his elbow, lowering his honeyed hand down into it. He screamed.

Trying to wrench himself free, he couldn't. Incontestable strength held his arm steady while sharp teeth bit out gobbets of his palm, savaged the marrow from his cracked fingerbones. Aqib kicked the stool away in his frenzy, and so hung for a long time against the glass, supported mid-air by teeth and only teeth, which rent and ground upon his hand. At length the agony ended, suddenly gone even beyond recall. His arm was loosed. Aqib fell down amidst the dust and coins, the bony debris. Fearfully he drew up his arm, peering in the gloom to examine his wound.

Weeping gore, a raw stump all thorned with bone-splinters? No. The end of his arm was smoothly sealed, just as scarless as if he'd never *had* a left hand, been born without.

"Now fuck off," the Sybil said. Aqib crouched down on all fours (three now) and crawled arduously back through the long narrow dimness of the tunnel, toward the outer light.

They'd awakened before dawn and climbed up the Sybil's Mount in a rush. One visit, on the appointed day, at the appointed hour: in a lifetime, one got no second chance. Aqib had crawled on alone through the deep tunnel, to live out the ordeal of a second life. Now, he emerged into sunlit mid-morning. First to catch sight of him was Lucrio.

He was nothing boyish anymore, everything distinguished, his brown hair shot through with silver, the laughlines deeply etched. Lucrio gave a cry no sooner than Aqib stuck his head from the tunnel's mouth. Then Olivy cried out too—Lucrio's niece whom they'd taken in some years back. She'd dallied with a god, and had to flee to them penniless and pregnant from her parents' fury. Four years old already, the baby jumped up. *Aqib-sa, Aqib-sa!* cried kohl-eyed Lucretius.

Aqib took in these faces. *Of course* home was here! The love hurt him it was so intense. He hadn't gone wrong in any sense, but rather found his very place, the one Saints had meant for him. Most would only ever guess at who and what was most precious to them—up until the day of loss: *then* they'd know—and most would also have to guess at why and how, or what might have been. They could never truly know, not as one who'd lived *both* paths, seen *two* lives. That crazed noise was his own laughter.

The hills of Daluz preened under the heights of Mt. Sibylline: shining white in late morning sun, the Cararian marble of the tenements, mansions and temples; the verdure, green and flowering, of the civil gardens and orchards of rich families; the whole, an orderly grid of streets and avenues. No sight possessed more wonderful powers to relieve, after having trudged with Lucrio some twenty years—through snow and mud, sand and forest—across the farflung provinces of Imperial Daluz. Now a general, now a governor, his lover had only lately been called home to the capitol, to assume Consulship.

Ecce homo: scrambling up the slope from the lower stony shelf where families waited for the supplicant gone within. Lucrio crushed him close in an embrace. "What happened? Are you leaving us?"

Beside himself, Aqib couldn't speak. He rolled his forehead side to side on Lucrio's shoulder, meaning, "No, of course not," but signifying quite ambiguously under the circumstances. Even as a shipwrecked sailor clings to his floating spar, so did he cling to Lucrio.

Finally Aqib found the breath to speak. "You said you'd tell me, once I came from the cave, what the Sybil told *you* so long ago."

Lucrio held him out at arm's length. "Are you leaving

me, Aqib?" First things first was Lucrio's tone. "Or will
you stay?"

"I want to stay for so long as you'll have me."

"Forever, then." Lucrio drew him back in close. "For
good. I asked the Sybil where in this world could I find
a man to love so well as the sailor I'd lost," Lucrio said in
Aqib's ear.

"Ah."

"She told me, 'Across the sea, in Olorum.' The Sybil
said, 'You'll glimpse him by moonlight walking not
alone, and you'll *know*, and yet also doubt. Maybe doubt
so much that he pass you by forever.'"

"But you called out to me from the fondac's door,"
Aqib said.

"Yes."

"And what coin did you pay the Sybil with, Lucrio?"

"With future tears. She said she'd be content to wait,
and then drink up all the tears I'd surely weep someday.
'Bitter tears are sweet to me,' the Sybil said," and Lucrio
quoted: "'You'll cry me an oceanful, I think. The likeliest
outcome is that you win your love for just a little while,
and then regret his loss forever. Yes, go. Seek him out. I
could happily wait upon such folly and sorrow. There's
every chance of grief.' But you can't imagine, Aqib, how
sick at heart I was in those days, before I met you. So I
went to Olorum."

"Do you know that I nearly refused to leave the Menagerie with you that day? I almost said, 'I'll come to you tonight.' But I would have been prevented, and this life we've lived together . . . I'm glad you persuaded me."

With difficulty Lucrio smiled, cheeks wet with tears. This was the first smile to emerge after a long and uncertain anguish, a smile possible only now that he might trust things could come out fine, after all. In Olorumi Lucrio said, "I'm glad about that too!"

Mother and child had climbed up to join them. Little Lucretius seized onto Aqib's leg, saying, *Don't leave us. Won't you stay, Aqib-sa? Stay!*

Aqib scooped up the baby to perch on his strong arm, and kissed the boy's cheek. *Of course I'm staying! I wouldn't be anywhere else in the world.*

Yay! The boy embraced him round the neck. *I'm glad. Me too, Lucreti.*

Lover and niece stared at Aqib, still no one commenting on his missing hand. They behaved as if they'd always known him thus and didn't notice the lack.

"*Avuncule,*" said Olivy, "what are these strange noises you make? Since you come from the Sybil's cave, you can now *understand* the boy's babble?"

With her question, it was borne in on him that the god-provoked fluency he'd gained in the garden on that fateful day—in that other life—had somehow carried over into this one. The speech of all creatures was plain to Aqib. "But your son never babbles at all, *mea filia,*" he exclaimed, looking back and forth between Olivy and Lucrio. "It's only that he speaks in the language of swans!"

About the Author

KAI ASHANTE WILSON's story "Super Bass" can be read online at *Tor.com,* as can his novelette "The Devil in America," which was nominated for the Nebula, Shirley Jackson, and World Fantasy Awards. His story "Kaiju *maximus:* 'So Various, So Beautiful, So New'" is available online as well at Fantasy-magazine.com, and his story «*Légendaire.*» can be read in the anthology *Stories for Chip*. His debut novella, *The Sorcerer of the Wildeeps,* was nominated for the Locus and won the 2016 Crawford Award. Kai Ashante Wilson lives in New York City.

TOR·COM

Science fiction. Fantasy. The universe. And related subjects.

*

More than just a publisher's website, *Tor.com* is a venue for **original fiction, comics,** and **discussion** of the entire field of SF and fantasy, in all media and from all sources. Visit our site today—and join the conversation yourself.

CPSIA information can be obtained
at www.ICGtesting.com
Printed in the USA
LVHW03s0106130618
580545LV00003B/645/P